SAVAGE PURSUIT

Slocum jumped onto the pinto, digging his spurs into the animal's sides. The pony burst forward, into the heart of the valley. Lead slugs and feathered arrows whizzed over the tall man's head. He fell forward, grabbing the pinto's mane.

A war cry rose in front of him. Slocum saw an Apache riding straight for him on a dark pony. He lifted his Colt and fired. The warrior tumbled to the rocky ground.

Slocum's stomach turned over when he saw the wall of rock ahead of him.

The tall man stopped the pony and slid off its shiny back. Nothing to do but climb.

The slope was steep but he could hang onto the trees. Slocum pulled himself onto a short ledge that receded toward the summit of the peak.

The smell hit him first. He turned to look at the carnage. The sight of the massacred cavalrymen sickened and horrified the tall Georgian. But at the same time, he thought he saw his chance to escape the savages on his tail . . .

OTHER BOOKS BY JAKE LOGAN

JAKE LOGAN

SLOCUM'S FORTUNE

B

BERKLEY BOOKS, NEW YORK

SLOCUM'S FORTUNE

A Berkley Book / published by arrangement with
the author

PRINTING HISTORY
Berkley edition / May 1991

ISBN: 0-425-12737-0

A BERKLEY BOOK ® TM 757,375
Berkley Books are published by The Berkley Publishing Group,
200 Madison Avenue, New York, New York 10016.
The name "BERKLEY" and the "B" logo
are trademarks belonging to Berkley Publishing Corporation.

PRINTED IN THE UNITED STATES OF AMERICA

10 9 8 7 6 5 4 3 2 1

This book is dedicated to
the memory of
Coleman "Papaw" Hall.

1

John Slocum tipped back his wide-brimmed hat and then leaned forward in the saddle, resting his rough hands on the dull luster of the saddlehorn. A bothersome pain spread through his lower back. He stretched a little but the aching didn't go away. Slocum reined the chestnut gelding and climbed down from the saddle. The pain vanished as soon as his boots hit the ground.

Slocum drew a hot breath and reached for the large canteen that hung from the saddle on the gelding. He had brought an extra canteen for the arid country of eastern Arizona. Slocum figured he had to be in the Arizona Territory by now. The mountains of New Mexico were two days behind him. And he could see the impressions of fresh peaks on the western horizon, probably Bassetts Peak or another mountain with a name he couldn't remember.

The chestnut whinnied. It smelled the water. Slocum

1

cupped his calloused hand to give the mount a drink. Just a whistle-wetter for the strong animal. A bellyful would make the gelding sick.

Slocum sipped carefully himself.

He turned his green eyes to the horizon, trying to calculate true west. Slocum wasn't necessarily going to continue on in that direction, but it would be a good point of reference. A man with time on his hands, a man who drifted from one job to another, that man had a choice of roads to take.

Slocum wiped his face with cool water. The dust formed mud on his fingertips. He had been eating trail dirt for the better part of a month. He was running from Texas, fleeing trouble that he wanted to forget: violent trouble; bad trouble; outrunning the sheriff trouble.

Slocum gave the gelding another taste of water, then returned the canteen to his saddle. He studied the plain, thinking that he had not crossed the San Simon River yet. But it had to be close.

Slocum didn't want to turn north, because he would head straight into Apache country. Not that there had been much trouble with the Apaches, at least none that Slocum had heard of. Still, if an Apache caught you on his land, he could pretty much do whatever he wanted with you. Sometimes the Mescaleros could think of some bad medicine. No sense going north, he told himself.

Tucson lay due west. There might be work there, but Slocum wasn't in mind of a big town, not after the fiasco in El Paso. Too much law in a big town. A rough-looking trail rider from Georgia stood out on a main street. Sheriffs took notice and marshals checked their wanted posters. A man like Slocum had to lay low in places like Tucson.

He was left with south and southwest, since he sure as hell wasn't going back east. He figured he could hit the river and follow it for a while. He wanted to steer around Fort Bowie, maybe stop off at a tiny town called Dos Cabezas.

Slocum remembered a cantina in Dos Cabezas. *Two Heads*. He could never figure out why the place was called by that name. It didn't matter. There was food and tequila there, along with a Mexican girl who served it up.

He dug into his pockets. Slocum had sold his rifle to buy the gelding. He had three silver dollars left after the trade.

By hunting for food and avoiding chances to buy whiskey, the three dollars were still in his possession.

Slocum licked his lips. A man needed a rest once in a while, to be good to himself. Three dollars would buy a lot of beans and tequila. He could eat sopapias, the sweet biscuits that the girl filled with honey.

The tall man from Georgia flinched at the thought of biscuits and honey. Every morning of his life before the war, there had been cathead biscuits and fresh clover honey on the table for breakfast. Then it had all disappeared, when he left home to ride against the Union. Carpetbaggers took what remained. Slocum saw it all so clearly at times. The aching was like a death in the family—a man got over it, but he never forgot.

The gelding snorted, rousing him from his reverie.

"You ain't gettin' more water, Jazbow. You'll take sick and I'll be walkin' on my feet."

He turned his green eyes to the sky. It was late morning and pretty soon the midday sun would be baking his brain. If he could get to the river, he might find some shade. There he could rest a while and then ride on for Dos Cabezas, when the day cooled a little.

Slocum swung slowly into the saddle, settling back in, waiting for the pain to shoot up his spine. But the aching was gone. Something had loosened and relaxed.

He nudged the gelding into an easy walk.

The animal was steady for a while, until it smelled the river.

Slocum gave the mount its head, galloping toward the narrow, rock and sand trickle of the San Simon.

At the river, he found shade in some rocks. He watered the gelding in stages, making sure it didn't get sick. Slocum intended to rest, but then the clouds swept down from the north, covering the sun. Late May sometimes delivered rain to the rough country and that could bring flash floods to any river, even a shallow stream like the San Simon.

Thunder crackled in the distance.

Slocum glanced toward the gelding to watch the animal's reaction. He hated riding a horse that was spooked by lightning and thunder. Slocum didn't like being thrown from a frightened mount.

The chestnut was nervous, but not really loco.

Slocum decided to ride.

He let the gelding have its head in the cooler air, but he wasn't able to outrun the storm.

The sky emptied torrents of rain on him. He was soaked before he could climb into his worn slicker. Then the storm rolled away, leaving the plain steamy and hot again.

Slocum kept on, walking the gelding for a while.

The sun returned to bake him dry, forcing him to stop to rest his mount in the heat. Picking up again in the afternoon, he went southwest, hoping to reach Dos Cabezas before nightfall. Dusk beat him to the town.

Slocum considered stopping to camp. Dos Cabezas wasn't the kind of place that lit up the sky. He might miss it in the dark.

But something inside the tall man from Georgia kept him going, a separate sense that had developed from the years of trail riding. The town must be close. And maybe he wouldn't have to actually see it in order to find it.

After a while, the gelding snorted and lifted its nose to the wind. Slocum reached for his sidearm, a Colt .36 he had garnered in the rifle-for-the-gelding deal. He figured the animal smelled a coyote.

Slocum thumbed back the hammer of the Colt. He was a good enough shot to plug rabbits for dinner. A coyote wouldn't be a problem, since it would probably go around him, anyway.

Then Slocum smelled the woodsmoke himself. It had to be the fire from the cantina. A pot of beans probably bubbled over the flames. Homemade tequila burned a man's throat, but the demon brew could free him from his cares for a while.

Slocum relaxed the reins of the gelding. "Go on, Jazbow, you find Dos Cabezas for me. And don't be slow about it."

The gelding ran again.

Slocum reined back when he saw the adobe ruins ahead of him. He had forgotten about the old Indian grounds. Maybe he could sleep there for a while, after he had filled his belly and dulled his head. Two Heads. Did they call it that because the tequila made a man see double?

He walked the gelding through the broken heaps of adobe brick.

He could almost taste the beans and the fry bread. Maybe the Mexican woman would still be there. Slocum suddenly ached to spend the three dollars in his jeans, to squander the sum total of his life savings.

Then a woman's scream rose up from the ruins and Slocum's plans took an entirely different turn.

There was no doubt in Slocum's mind that the scream belonged to a woman. It was a short, high-pitched yelp that reverberated through the cool night. Slocum reined back the gelding and hesitated, listening.

The woman screamed again.

Slocum dismounted, trying to mark the direction of the noise. He heard whimpering and then a slapping sound. The woman continued to cry in muffled sobs.

Slocum drew a hand over the stubble on his chin. Maybe it would be best just to keep riding into Dos Cabezas. He didn't exactly need more trouble.

Another slapping sound penetrated the darkness. Then a man's voice came behind the woman's cry.

Slocum drew a deep breath. Despite his trail-hardened weariness, the tall man from Georgia had once been a Southern gentleman, the kind of man who didn't take much to slapping women. The distress call of a weak, helpless woman roused something in Slocum that would never die. He decided to have a look.

Guiding the chestnut to a stretch of flat, adobe wall, Slocum used the stirrup for a lift. He climbed onto the saddle and then onto the crest of the wall. When he had gained his balance, he squared his shoulders and swung his head in a wide circle.

The man's voice became clearer from the higher vantage point. He was speaking in Spanish. Slocum couldn't understand what he was saying, but the rugged trail rider knew the tone of anger.

His eyes tried to pierce the shadows of the moonless night. For a moment, Slocum thought he wasn't going to see them. Then something moved in the shaded dent between the adobe ruins.

"Puta!"

Slocum knew that word. It meant whore in Spanish. He watched as the man dragged the woman a few feet and threw her to the ground.

Slocum's hand dropped to the butt of the Colt .36 on his side. He still hadn't decided if he wanted to get involved. Maybe they were married. Even a gentleman didn't come between a husband and his woman.

The man kept talking in Spanish, entreating the woman to tell him something he wanted to know. She seemed to deny the knowledge he had in mind. So he grabbed her arms and pulled her up again, shaking her, striking her.

The woman begged pitifully for him to stop, but the man was adamant. He threatened more harm, maybe even death.

Slocum exhaled and drew his Colt, thumbing back the hammer.

"I think she's had enough," he said in the darkness.

The vaquero froze where he stood. He glanced to his right and his left and then looked behind himself. The woman also turned her head to look for the voice that might be her salvation.

Slocum watched the man, waiting for him to pull a sidearm. But his hands stayed on the woman. And the tall man's Colt stayed on him.

"You might oughta let her go," Slocum said. "She might tell you what you wanna know if you stop slappin' her."

The man's eyes turned upward to the shadow that stood on the wall. He let go of the woman. She slipped back into the shadows.

"This is no worry of yours, señor."

Mexican, Slocum thought.

The man's hands started to fall toward his side.

"I wouldn't do that," Slocum advised. "Keep your palms high. Let me see that white hand."

"Keel heem!" the woman cried.

The Mexican told her to shut up in Spanish.

Slocum held steady with the Colt. "He your husband, ma'am?"

"No. He ees peeg. *Puerco!*"

The Mexican made a move toward her.

Slocum stopped him with a harsh word. The man froze

again. Slocum stayed still himself, wondering what the next move would be. What the hell had he gotten himself into? He hadn't been in town for five minutes and he had already brewed up a passel of trouble. He sure as hell didn't want to shoot the Mexican. They just stood there for a couple of seconds.

Then the Mexican made it easy for him. He turned and started to run away, disappearing quickly into the shadows. The woman gave a cry of relief.

Slocum held the Colt in hand for a few minutes, staying on his perch at the top of the wall, waiting to see if the Mexican's departure had been some kind of trick. But the vaquero did not fire his gun. And when Slocum heard the horse galloping away to the south, he knew the trouble was over—at least for a while. He holstered the .36 and climbed down onto the back of the gelding.

The lanky Georgian figured to just ride on into town, find that bottle of tequila and maybe a cornshuck mattress for the night. No need to hang around the woman any longer. He had finished her misery for her. And he had every reason to believe that the Mexican would probably be back to find what he was looking for. Best just to get through Dos Cabezas and keep riding south in the morning.

But the woman had other ideas.

As Slocum guided the chestnut out of the adobe ruins, he heard her calling to him in English. She was thanking him, begging him not to run away. Then she was there, running beside him, grabbing his leg.

Slocum reined back on the gelding. "Let it go, señorita."

"Señor, please! You help me. Please."

Slocum shook his head, figuring it had been a bad mistake to get involved in the fracas between the man and the woman. And the only way to right the wrong was to put a hundred miles between him and Dos Cabezas. Forget that he had ever been there. Maybe head for the border of Mexico. Things might be more comfortable on the other side.

"Señor! I weel geeve you wha' you wan'. Food, wheesky!"

Slocum sighed. "Look here, woman, your beau is liable to come a courtin' again and he's not gonna take it kindly if I'm here."

"No," she insisted, "he won' come back. No tonigh'."
She clung tightly to his leg.

Slocum might have ridden on, had he not caught a whiff of
her perfume. It wasn't the kind of whore-water that Mexican
girls usually wore. The scent reminded him of the fine ladies
he had once known in Atlanta, where he had experienced a
life that had long since disappeared.

"Please, señor!"

He considered the bad end of things. What if the vaquero
did return tonight? And what if he brought a bunch of his
compañeros? Slocum didn't even have a rifle.

"Look here, woman—"

"Rosita. My name ees Rosita. Please, señor. I have food
and tequila. You weel see the cantina ees dark tonigh'."

Slocum gazed toward town, which was barely a dark lump
on the horizon. No lights at all burned in Dos Cabezas, not
even a single oil lamp. The woman's offer suddenly didn't
look so bad. He could eat and drink, then move on in the
darkness.

"All right," he said softly. "Point me toward the stew-
pot."

"Gracias, señor."

She put her cheek against his leg, hugging him.

Slocum moved the chestnut so she would have to let go.
Before he could say anything else, Rosita grabbed the reigns
of the mount, pulling the chestnut through the cool shadows. Slocum's hand immediately dropped back to the butt
of the Colt Navy, anticipating an ambush in the darkness.
But Rosita only led him to an orange circle of embers that
glowed under an iron pot.

He watched from the saddle as she threw fat kindling onto
the fire. Yellow flames rose up instantly. Slocum swung his
green eyes from side to side, watching for bushwhackers in
the fresh circle of light.

Rosita's round face turned toward him. "There ees no
danger, señor. No more tonigh'."

Slocum figured she was telling the truth. He dismounted
and drew closer to the fire. The plain, hot in the day, could
be cold at night. The heat relieved some of the stiffness in
his body.

Rosita moved around to stir the iron pot.

For the first time, Slocum got a good look at her face. She was beautiful. Too beautiful to be in trouble in a place like Dos Cabezas. Beautiful enough to cause more misery than Slocum wanted to deal with on a cold, godforsaken Arizona night.

2

Rosita spooned up a wooden bowl full of the dark stew and handed it to Slocum. She reached into a cloth bag to pull out a hunk of corn bread. Slocum crumbled the dried cake into the stew and stirred it a couple of times. The gravy tasted of salt and onions. Slocum didn't bother to ask what kind of meat the girl had used. It was gamey, like rabbit or ringtail.

She dished up a portion for herself.

Slocum watched her from the corner of his eye. She ate like a village girl, slurping hungrily from the wooden bowl. The black dress she wore was shiny and creased, with a white frilly lace circle at her throat. A village woman who had made good somewhere along the way, Slocum thought. She was so damned beautiful that she had more than likely married a man with some money.

Her black eyes turned toward him. The fire glinted in her

irises. Thick lips parted. She looked away.

Slocum pushed his empty bowl toward her. "Good stew."

Without a word, Rosita filled his bowl again.

"Don't want to take all your food," Slocum said. "One bowl's enough."

She sighed disgustedly, like she was tired of all men and their stupid troubles. "Eat. I ha' people here. They ha' no forgotten me."

Slocum didn't want to be impolite. Besides, his belly wasn't full yet. And a man on the ride could never be sure when he'd have another meal that wasn't a rabbit on a stick over a campfire. He tried to eat slowly but the stew tasted of those good Mexican chili peppers.

Rosita put her empty bowl on the ground. "Your name, señor?"

Slocum's green eyes narrowed. "Ain't sure I want you to know my name."

"No?"

"You got troubles," the tall man replied. "Not that every soul don't have its share of grief. Your trouble ain't mine and I don't want it to be."

"You chase Miguel away," Rosita said. "He ha' compañeros. He weel ride to find you."

"Maybe. But he'll have a harder time of it if he doesn't know my name. And he won't come far, not as far as I plan to go."

She sighed. "You are smart, señor. Like the fox. And you will be smart to leave Dos Cabezas."

He doubted the truth of her reference to the Mexican man's compañeros. She was just trying to pull him into it. Rosita needed somebody on her side, but Slocum didn't want the details. He could get a couple of hours in the bedroll and clear out of Dos Cabezas before dawn.

There was still some unfinished business. "You said somethin' about whiskey, señorita."

Rosita reached into the cloth bag and brought out a bottle of murky cactus juice. She tossed it casually to Slocum. The tall man popped the cork, lifting it to his lips, drinking, waiting for the burn in his throat. But it went down smoothly. His tongue felt a little raw, like the roof of his mouth. But there was no fire in his gullet, no explosion in the pit of his belly.

After a few more slugs, he began to feel the glow inside him. Replacing the cork, he handed the bottle back to Rosita.

"Ha' more," she offered.

Slocum shook his head. He didn't want to have an aching skull when he woke up. He knew just when to stop.

Rosita put the bottle back in the cloth bag. Her black eyes focused on the lanky drifter from Georgia. He wasn't the kind of man a woman would call handsome, although his face had a rugged quality that Rosita found interesting. He wasn't young, but he hadn't gotten old yet. He had seen things; it showed in the lines of his face. Rosita had seen things herself. And she wanted to talk about it.

"Señor, you no ass why Miguel heet me."

Slocum sighed, reaching into his shirt pocket. "Ain't no reason for me to ask. Damn."

His tobacco pouch was empty. No chance to roll a cigarette after the food and the liquor. Sometimes a man couldn't have everything he needed.

Rosita reached into her cloth bag again. "Ha' thees."

She tossed him a black tin of tobacco. Slocum recognized the brand from his days back East. It was good, North Carolina leaf. He quickly rolled a fat one and started to close the tin.

"Feel your pouch," the girl told him.

Slocum squinted at her. "I ain't sure—"

"Do eet. I don' wan notheen' from you, señor. I took eet fra' Miguel. To make heem loco."

Slocum didn't argue. He stuffed his pouch full. The girl was being fair with him, paying him back for chasing the man away.

Slocum began to feel a little uneasy about the man called Miguel. The Mexican obviously had some geetus. Good tobacco and fancy dresses for his peasant girl. Rosita had left him for some other reason.

That round, dark face turned toward Slocum in the firelight. She had to be shy of her twentieth birthday. He felt sorry for her.

"You got people?" he asked.

She nodded.

"Why ain't you with 'em?"

A tear rolled out of her eye. "Miguel deed no marry me.

Hees father would no let heem. My people weel help me, but they weel no tay me back."

Slocum had seen it before. Peasants, poor farmers, sod-busters—they were usually people of principle. They didn't have to become cheats and carpetbaggers like men of means. They had nothing to lose by sticking to their beliefs. Rosita had been an adultress in the eyes of her family, so they could no longer welcome her back home.

He decided not to ask her where she was going or what she planned to do. It would be easier to leave if he didn't have a personal stake in her troubles. Sometimes women could be hard to resist if they needed a hand. Especially for a rough-face son of the Confederacy like Slocum. A Southern man was raised to do right by women.

"Miguel weel no come back," Rosita said as she wiped her eyes. "Hees father, Don Franceesco, weel no let heem marry me."

Slocum just pulled at the butt of the hand-roll.

"Señor, where are you going?"

"No place you want to ride, señorita. I'm just driftin'. Lookin' for an honest day's work. I don't s'pose there's anythin' like that in Dos Cabezas."

"There's work," she replied. "For a pistolero."

Slocum leaned back, stubbing out the butt. Gunfighting wasn't really his line, even though he seemed to find plenty of chances to use his Colt. He had killed men, in the war and since. But he had never relished it the way some men did. A true pistolero seemed to enjoy killing.

"Miguel fancies heemself a pistolero," Rosita went on. "But you saw how fast he ran. He ees a coward."

"That why you left him?" Slocum wondered if he would regret the question.

Rosita stared out into the darkness. "I know many sins, señor. But I could sin no more. No more."

He figured to let it rest.

But she wanted to talk. "Señor, where can I go?"

Slocum shrugged, feeling uncomfortable with all the chatter. "Tucson, Tombstone maybe. Santa Fe."

Rosita started to cry again, to really sob. She got up, running away from the fire, away from Slocum. He breathed a little easier with her gone. No need to chase her. He wanted to get some sleep and get the hell out of Dos Cabezas.

Women had a way of making a man stay in a place and Slocum knew better than to fall into the same old trap. Rosita had left her man because he was doing something she couldn't abide. There was lots of shady business along the border, Mexican and gringo. Slocum wondered if he was really better off not knowing about the man she called Miguel. Sometimes a scrap of information could save a man's life. It might help him steer clear of a gunfight.

He heard her coming back toward him.

Slocum stood up, heading for his mount, unsaddling the chestnut. He had to lay a bedroll for the night. Rosita was by the fire when he returned. She would not look at him as he fixed his bed.

"Only got but one blanket," he offered, "but you're welcome to it."

She shook her head, saying that she had blankets.

Slocum reclined on the bedroll, using his saddle for a pillow. He felt bad that he couldn't help the girl more, but that was how it fell sometimes. A man had to resist making trouble for himself, even if he could smell that sweet perfume.

He pulled his hat over his eyes, falling asleep, waking when the girl slid down next to him on the blanket.

Slocum opened his eyes, staring up at the purple steel glow of the Arizona sky. It was already daybreak. He had slept too long.

The girl's perfume filled his nostrils. Her head lay on his chest and her hand rubbed his stomach. Slocum figured the smart thing was to shut it off right then, but he didn't feel so smart as her hand slid down to his crotch.

He touched her thick hair. She moaned, knowing that he was awake. Her fingers began to work on the buttons of his fly.

The tall man felt flesh on flesh. Her touch stroked away a multitude of sorrows that would take a while to return. Slocum had been blessed with the carnal company of a woman, an ancient balm that could cure most of a man's ails, at least temporarily.

Rosita shifted next to him, lifting the hem of her black

dress. He felt her weight as she swung a leg over. Her face looked down at him.

Slocum grabbed her, pressing his mouth to hers. Rosita returned the kiss with a probing tongue. She writhed on top of him, rubbing his body with her own, guiding a hand to her breast.

Slocum touched the smoothness of her backside with his other hand. She rolled her hips, feeling his prick between her thighs, rubbing her wetness against his probing hardness.

"You taste like wheesky!" she whispered.

He thrust his hips, trying to enter her.

"No," Rosita said. "Let me."

She sat up, straddling him, using her legs like springs. Her broad bottom rotated over the spire of his erection. In one motion, she sat on him, taking him in.

Slocum closed his eyes. She must have been a whore at one time. Where else would she have learned so well what a man wanted?

Rosita leaned forward a little, picking up her pace. She moved like a desert cat, rolling her head as she found her own pleasure. Slocum began to swell inside her. She lurched forward, falling on top of him, kissing him as he discharged inside her.

They took a while to catch their breaths.

Rosita rolled off him, pulling down her dress. She told him she could not help herself. She had been used to getting it every night.

Slocum wasn't complaining. He put his arm around her shoulder.

She nuzzled into his chest. "Say me your name."

Slocum exhaled dejectedly. There it was, the final draw, the showdown, cards on the table. She wanted to know who he was. She knew he would not be able to deny her after they had shared the bedroll.

He wanted to tell her because he had loved her, if only for a few minutes. "Slocum."

"Slocum. Where you fra', Slocum?"

"Place called Georgia. It's east. In the south. South of the Mason-Dixon line. Only—hell, I been gone so long, I'm not even sure it's still there."

She sighed a little. "Why you co' here?"

"'Cause there's no north or south when you cross the Mississippi. Just west and plenty of it."

"I theen I go to Santa Fe," Rosita offered. "They got Mexicans there?"

Slocum nodded. He knew he had said too much already. He planned to go in the opposite direction. He still couldn't shake the feeling that she was trouble.

Rosita's hand returned to the softness between his legs. Her fingers began to work again. Slocum wasn't sure he would be able, but his worries disappeared quickly. It might be a while before he lucked into another woman like Rosita. Best to take advantage of it while it was there.

He pushed her onto her back. "Unbutton that dress." He said it softly, a request rather than an order.

Rosita's fingers were fast. She pulled back the top portion of her dress, revealing the brown ends of her breasts. Slocum kissed her nipples, licking the taut circles.

She lifted her dress again and spread her legs.

Slocum fell between her thighs, prodding her, trying to pierce the wetness with the tip of his cock.

Rosita arched her back and then guided him in. "Hard," she told him.

Slocum shook her, discharging, driving her into her own release. She held him tightly within her. He lay on top of her, ready to sleep again.

When he tried to roll off, she moaned. "Noo. No, Miguel."

Slocum tensed. "I'm not Miguel."

"No, I—"

He fell onto his bedroll again.

Rosita put her hand on his chest. "I am sorry, señor."

He touched her hair, stroking the back of her head. "Let it go. I'm not your man and you're not my woman. We just got stuck in Dos Cabezas on the wrong night. No more or less."

She sat up, glaring at him, pulling down her dress. "Señor loco! Loco hombre!" She began to curse in Spanish.

Slocum hitched up his pants and then leaned back against the saddle. His eyes were heavy. In spite of the girl's ranting, he wanted to sleep again. If he was lucky, he wouldn't dream.

He opened his eyes a little, just to look at the sky. There was a predawn glow, but the sun had not made it over the eastern horizon. He might be able to nap another hour and then get started after daybreak.

Rosita made noise as she tossed kindling onto the last embers of the fire. She nursed the sparks into flame. Slocum wondered if she would make breakfast for him. Probably not.

Maybe he should help her. For a moment, between sleep and waking, he considered taking her to Santa Fe. Maybe she had some money and could pay him for his effort. He wouldn't have minded sharing a bedroll with her all the way back to New Mexico.

He shook off the dumb notion. His better judgment told him to head southwest. If nothing else, he could end up in Yuma or maybe Nogales. He had to find some work soon. The three dollars in his pocket were not going last forever. It would all go as soon as he hit a town.

Rosita started moving again. Slocum lifted his head and watched as she walked toward his mount. At first he thought she was going to steal the gelding, but she only slipped an oat bag over its head. Slocum had to give her credit; she was a damned thoughtful woman.

Rosita saw him looking at her. She pouted and turned back to the fire. He couldn't take her south, not back toward the trouble she had left.

What if he met her boyfriend on the trail? No, Miguel would not recognize him. It had been too dark when Slocum drew down on the Mexican. And he was pretty sure the girl had already forgotten his name. He had only told her once.

If things didn't work out in Arizona, he could always push on to Nevada or California.

Slocum leaned back and closed his eyes. Sometimes it felt so good to sleep. One of life's simple pleasures. At least until he woke up to what seemed to be an earthquake.

3

After a couple of seconds, Slocum realized that it wasn't an earthquake causing the thunder and dust. Nor was it a storm from the clear, bright morning sky. Hooves pounded the ground on both sides of him, raising billows of chalky grit as the animals rushed around the adobe ruins.

Horses or cows, Slocum thought, or both.

He stood up, looking for the girl. But Rosita was no longer there. Had she taken his horse?

Slocum started forward to look for the gelding. He stopped cold when his ears detected the shouts and whistles of men rising above the beastly din. What if Rosita's boyfriend had come back to even the score? He would bring compañeros with him, many guns against one.

He had sure as hell stayed too long in Dos Cabezas.

The gelding whinnied across the way, rearing, trying to pull away from its tether. Slocum started for the animal. As he ran over the dry ground, a dogie burst out of nowhere, shooting between Slocum and the gelding. The steer turned to look at him. Slocum picked up a rock and sent the cow on its path back to the herd.

Slocum grabbed the reins of the gelding and tried to steady it. The thundering kept up all around him. How many steers were there? It seemed to be a pretty big herd.

More cattle ran in and out of the ruins as Slocum saddled the chestnut. If Rosita's boyfriend had returned, the tall man's best chance was to run. Maybe there wouldn't be any trouble. Nothing dangerous about a herd of cattle.

He managed to break camp, tying his bedroll at the rear of his saddle.

Still the cows kept moving past him. There must have been a thousand head. Where the hell had such a big herd come from in Arizona? Slocum had never known this parched borderland to be cattle country.

Cowboys whistled and yelled, closer than Slocum wanted them to be. He tried to pull the gelding into the shadows between the old walls, but the chestnut fought him, rearing and snorting.

Slocum saw a man on horseback. The cowboy came and went in the corner of his eye. Had he seen Slocum? The cowboy disappeared on the other side of the ruins.

Slocum felt like running, but he knew they would see him the minute he climbed into the saddle. He had to get into cover. Removing his hat, he used it to cover the gelding's eyes. When the chestnut was blinded, he dragged it between two narrow walls, barely fitting into the cool shadows.

Something moved behind him. Slocum drew the Colt Navy as he turned. He stuck the barrel in the face of a pretty woman.

"Rosita!"

She threw her arms around his waist, burying her face in his chest.

Slocum stood there, his Colt in hand, listening as the dull thunder began to fade. Another steer rushed by them, followed by a cowboy who hesitated for a moment, looking into the shadows where Slocum stood with the girl. The rider was dressed like a gringo. He moved on before Slocum could fret about him.

"Deed he see us?" Rosita asked.

Slocum grimaced. "I don't know. He one of your boyfriend's men?"

She shook her head. "These are no' Miguel's men."

"You sure about that?"

Rosita pushed away from him, her face drawn up in an angry expression. "I wan' to tell you las' night, but you no let me."

Slocum lifted a finger. "Shh."

He heard two voices. They were calling back in forth in English.

"Any strays?"

"Don't see none."

"Check the adobe."

"Aw."

"Go on."

"They're comin' in," Slocum said.

But he turned to see that Rosita had disappeared again. She had scurried through a hole in the bricks. If they weren't her lover's compañeros, why was she running?

The gelding whinnied.

Slocum put the hat over its eyes. He stayed motionless, waiting for the rider to find him. The cowboys might be friendly, but Slocum still wanted to avoid them if he could. He just wanted to get south in a hurry.

A shape rushed in front of him. Slocum held his breath. It was only a steer. But then the cowboy came right behind it.

"Get on there, beefsteak," the rider called. "You're in the army, you worthless side of meat. Hy-yah!"

The steer bawled and rushed out of the ruins. Slocum listened as the rider kept moving. Again the horse came even with his hiding place. The rider stared into the shadows, peering right at Slocum. Did he see the tall man back there?

Slocum breathed easier when the rider moved on. He listened as the roar of hooves grew fainter. The wranglers moved the herd into Dos Cabezas, down the main street of the dirty little town.

Dust still swirled in the air. Slocum moved through the grit, leading the gelding. He figured the coast was clear. Then the girl appeared at his side, coming from nowhere.

"They din' see me," Rosita offered.

Slocum felt a chill in his shoulders. "Good for you."

Rosita touched his arm. "Don' you wan' to know where those cows came fra', señor?"

His green eyes glared at her. "What's my name, Rosita?"

"Huh?"

Then she had forgotten. Slocum wanted to keep it that way. He bent to check the cinch of his saddle one more time before he rode off.

"Señor?" She grabbed his arm.

Slocum gently removed her grip. She dropped to her knees, grabbing his legs, hugging him, pleading with him to stay. He had to shake her off.

"I can't help you, señorita."

He put one foot in the stirrup.

"You are a coward!" she cried. "Like Miguel."

Slocum hesitated. He didn't like being called a coward. The word made a man think. It made a man want to prove himself, like in the war. Every man going into battle had his fears and doubts. The only difference between a coward and a hero was the way they acted in the face of danger.

"Don' leave me, cowboy!"

Slocum looked back at her, cursing the accidental meeting. He should have ridden past Dos Cabezas in the night, pushed on to Nogales. The cantina owners in Nogales would have been glad to take his three dollars.

"Those cows," he said, "your boyfriend has somethin' to do with 'em?"

Rosita nodded.

"That's all I needed to know."

Slocum swung into the saddle.

"Coward!"

"No. Just not ready for fights that aren't mine."

Rosita rushed to him, wrapping her arms around his leg. "Don' go, señor. Please. Stay wi' me."

She continued to plead, but Slocum managed to resist. Leaving was the best thing. The trouble didn't belong to him. He hadn't caused it and he had no reason to end it. He brushed off Rosita, urging the chestnut toward the open plain. He figured to have seen the last of her and Dos Cabezas. But he was dead wrong on both counts.

The gelding stepped gingerly through the ruins. Slocum had to take it slow. He didn't want the chestnut stepping on a rock and coming up lame.

Nogales lay ahead for the tall man. Maybe if he got there quickly enough, he could forget about the girl. He felt guilty about not helping her, but he knew he would get over it.

The chestnut whinnied.

Slocum patted the animal's neck. "Easy."

It was still nervous from the unexpected arrival of the herd.

Slocum urged the gelding out of the ruins. He stopped for a moment to gaze back toward Dos Cabezas. A dusty cloud hung over the small town. He had never made it to the cantina, thanks to the charity of the Mexican girl. He almost turned back to her, but he thought twice about it and decided to leave for the border.

As he turned the gelding to the southwest, Slocum heard the rattling of rifle levers. The riders were hanging inside the adobe ruins, close to where he had been hiding. Slocum considered running to his right, but another rider came out of the dust.

Three of them held Winchesters on him.

"Don't move, pardner."

"Raise those hands high."

"He's got a pistol."

Slocum wanted to take a chance, to make a break. But he knew one of the three rifles would get lucky at this range, even if he was moving like the wind. So the tall, green-eyed Georgian lifted his palms to the dusty sky, waiting for them to take him.

A tall man in a high Stetson guided a gray horse toward Slocum. He studied the drifter with narrow brown eyes. The other riflemen hung back, keeping their rifles on Slocum even as the high-hat dropped the barrel of his Winchester.

"What you doin' hidin' back there?" the man asked.

Slocum shrugged. "Just campin' for the night. Rode into town too late for the cantina."

No need to tell them about the girl.

"Anybody with ya?"

Slocum shook his head. "No. Ridin' alone. Reckon I got in the way of your dogies. For that I say I'm sorry."

One of the riders laughed. "He looks like a sorry one, all right."

The high-hatted man glared at the rifleman. "Put down that iron and don't make fun of this boy. Any one of you saddle bums has been in this man's boots more'n once."

He looked back at Slocum and smiled, which made the tall man like him immediately. As the riflemen lowered their Winchesters, Slocum asked if he could lower his hands. The high-hat nodded.

"Name's Garrity," the high-hat said. "Just Garrity. What they call you, stranger?"

Slocum hesitated.

The arrogant rider chortled again. "Prob'ly got posters on him strewed from here to Texas."

Garrity threw another harsh look at the rifleman. "I s'pose you never had a poster on you, Rattman."

Rattman had a vicious, dirty look about him. His hand opened and closed on the grip of the rifle. Dark eyes burned right through Slocum. He acted like he wanted to shoot somebody.

Slocum looked back at Garrity. He was clearly the leader.

Garrity motioned Rattman and the other rider toward Dos Cabezas. When Rattman didn't move right away, Garrity shot him another harsh glare.

Rattman bristled at Slocum and then rode off toward the herd.

Garrity sighed. "He's a rough one. But you look like a rough one, too, pardner. You want to tell me what to call you?"

Slocum glanced southward, over Garrity's shoulder. "If I'm ridin' on, no need for you to call me at all."

"Like to know a man's name if I'm gonna offer him a job," Garrity replied. "You interested in some work?"

"Depends on the kind of work you're offerin'." Slocum figured he could at least hear the man out.

"It's honest work," Garrity went on. "If you consider wranglin' honest. You run cows before?"

Slocum nodded.

"Like it?" Garrity asked.

"You ever know anybody to like wranglin'?"

Garrity laughed, even though Slocum hadn't meant to be funny. "I reckon you got a point there."

Garrity guided the gray around Slocum, reining back to look north. Dust stirred in the hot air. It was going to be a scorcher of a day. Early summer heat could be hell on a herd of cows.

"Takin' up to Pima," Garrity offered. "Figure to reach the San Simon and follow it all the way."

Slocum nodded, as if to say that wasn't a bad way to go. Although the tall man had no real desire to head north, he answered honestly because Garrity was no longer a threat.

"Gonna sell this bunch to the army," Garrity went on in his talkative manner. "I reckon they're gonna feed 'em to the Indians. Got the big reservation up that way."

Slocum frowned a little. If the cows were going to the army, why weren't they taking them to Fort Bowie? Of course, Pima was closer to the Apache land, but as a former army man, Slocum knew that no military logic ever made things simple. Still, it wasn't his trouble, just like the girl.

He glanced over his shoulder, wondering if Rosita had fled from the ruins. She had said something about the cattle, like she knew where they were going. How the hell had she known unless her boyfriend, Miguel, was in on the deal somehow?

"I'm three men short for a herd like this," Garrity said.

Slocum nodded toward the dusty cloud. "What about those two?"

Garrity made a scoffing noise. "Rattman's good with a gun, but he doesn't know what's what with cows. No sir, I could use a wrangler who's punched cattled before—"

"Mr. Garrity, I don't think I—"

"Pays ten dollars a day," Garrity offered.

Slocum winced. The cattle had to be stolen if this man was offering such a steep day wage. A cowboy usually earned a dollar a day, flat and unnegotiable. Take it or leave it.

"Gonna take at least five days to get those cows to Pima," Garrity said. "Fifty dollars for you, pardner. And you don't look like the kind of man who can pass that up."

Garrity had him there. A man in Slocum's position might take two months to earn fifty dollars. And he'd have to do it by shoveling shit or digging fence post holes. Fifty dollars was a temptation, even if the herd had been stolen and run up from Mexico.

And who would complain about Mexican cows on this side of the border? Hell, if the army didn't care where the herd came from, then why should Slocum? He could taste the fifty dollars. That much money might sustain him for three or four months if he stayed away from the saloon.

Garrity seemed to read the signs of the tall man's wavering. "I know what you're thinkin', pardner. Those cows are stolen. Well, they might be. But they were stolen on this side of the border, so nobody's gonna do a thing about it."

"How come you're not payin' the regular wage, Garrity? Ten a day is banker's money. And I sure as hell ain't no banker."

"Gover'ment's payin' us a passel for these cows. Had to bring 'em quick. Been some trouble up that way with an Injun name of Red Buck. Army figgers to settle him down with some fresh beef."

Slocum saw some sense in that line of reasoning, but he hadn't heard a thing about an Apache named Red Buck. Of course, he hadn't been in the territory long enough to pick up the local gossip. A man who rode alone wasn't always privy to news of the region.

And he was thinking of that ten dollars a day. What if Garrity had offered the steep pay only to cheat him later? The man seemed to read his mind. Garrity took out a shiny ten-dollar gold piece. He held it up so it sparkled in the sun.

Slocum couldn't deny the lure of the money.

"First day's wage in advance," Garrity said.

Slocum felt his head nodding. Garrity threw him the coin. Slocum caught it and studied it closely, making sure it was real.

"I'll go as far as Pima," Slocum said. "No more."

Garrity smiled. "Fine by me, pardner."

"John. Call me John."

"Lot of men named John in this terr'tory."

Slocum frowned. "Now there's one more."

Garrity laughed again. "Come on, pardner. Let's get back to the herd." He spurred the gray into the dust.

Slocum started to follow. He stopped for an instant before he spurred the gelding. His green eyes stared back at the ruins. Slocum could swear he heard the woman laughing. He turned the chestnut north, riding in a direction he had not really wanted to go. But at ten dollars a day, a working man was liable to do a few things that went against his better nature.

4

Garrity had been right about one thing—the trail drive was definitely short-handed. Besides the leering man named Rattman, Slocum had to ride with Rattman's partner—who lived up to the monicker of Shorty—Garrity himself, and two other wranglers who seemed to have most of the cowboying experience.

Bill and Cal had the look of young men seeking their fortune in the West. Still, their wrangling skills were true-hearted, if somewhat rusty. As soon as Slocum joined the drive, it was apparent to all that the tall man had worked cattle before. He impressed them by cutting back three strays and then roping a bull that had been giving them some trouble. Slocum threw the lariat around the old bull's horns, dragging him to the head of the drive, making him lead so he'd be too tired to get nasty.

Garrity galloped up next to Slocum, smiling at the tall

man. "Good work. What else should we do?"

Slocum knew then that Garrity wasn't a cattleman. Probably, the round-faced man had been hired as a regulator, a middle wheel in the bargain. He was awfully quick to trust Slocum—a man who wanted to get things done so he could rake the payoff at the end of the deal.

Slocum looked back at Rattman and his partner, Shorty. They leered at Slocum, even more angry at his superior skills. Some men just had a lot of hate in them. It was something a good man had to get used to.

"Those two are worthless," Slocum said.

Garrity laughed, tipping back his ten-gallon hat. "Say it twice and I'll agree with you. Like tits on a bull. Useless."

Slocum shot him a green-eyed look of agression. "Mind tellin' me why you need so much iron?"

The chubby Garrity took off the hat and wiped a head of gray and black hair. He was dressed like a townsman: white shirt, dark vest, good pants. He frowned and looked north, squinting at the horizon.

"I won't lie to you, John. Injuns up that way been kinda skittish lately. I want to get in and get out fast, but in case we don't, I like to have somebody along who can shoot. And I see you don't have a rifle."

Slocum looked away. "No, I don't."

Garrity had two Winchesters on his sling ring. "Here, take this one. Shoots a little to the left."

Slocum accepted the weapon. It was pretty clean, oiled and ready to fire. He asked if he could buy the rifle. Garrity said it would count as one day's pay. He also told Slocum to have the firing pin checked as soon as he could get the Winchester to a gunsmith.

The tall man from Georgia felt better as he slipped the rifle into the empty scabbard on his saddle.

"You're already twenty dollars ahead," Garrity remarked with a laugh.

Slocum gestured back to Rattman and Shorty. "Put 'em on drag," he said. "They'll eat some dust, but it won't be hard. They just have to keep the herd movin' and whistle when they spot strays."

"What about Bill and Cal?"

Slocum looked over his other shoulder. The younger men

were stationed on the sides of the herd, one on the right and one on the left. Slocum told Garrity to let them be. Slocum would assume responsibility for cutting back the strays and keeping the herd in the right direction.

"Then you're trail boss," Garrity said. "Anybody says diff'rent, you send 'em to me."

Slocum didn't want to be trail boss, but before he could protest, Garrity rode back to tell Rattman and Shorty to ride drag. Slocum watched over his shoulder as Rattman bristled. He argued with Garrity, but the chubby man finally won. Rattman glowered one last time at Slocum and then rode to the rear of the herd. Shorty followed reluctantly.

Garrity then rode to the younger men, telling them that they had to do as Slocum said. Both of them rubbernecked, gazing forward. Slocum waved a flat hand to let them know they were fine. They both nodded as if they didn't mind taking orders.

Slocum turned forward again. How the hell had he ended up as trail boss? The cattle had to be stolen, otherwise Garrity would not be in such a hurry to get them north. Maybe somebody from south of the border was on his trail.

Rustling was a crime in the Arizona Territory. A man could hang for stealing another man's herd. But the same rule didn't seem to apply for cows that were "found" in Mexico. It wasn't stealing if you hit a Mexican ranchero and brought his cows over the border.

Slocum heard whistling from behind. He looked back to see a group of steers as they veered away from the rest of the herd. Immediately, he turned the chestnut and started after the strays.

The Texas-bred gelding had once been a cowboy's mount. It knew how to cut steers in and out. Slocum only had to let it go. In a few minutes, the errant dogies were back in the main body of the herd.

Slocum started for point again. He felt the rider drawing next to him. He glanced over, expecting to see Garrity. Instead, Rattman's black eyes stared back at him.

Rattman wasn't the kind of man Slocum would have liked under any circumstances. Swarthy-faced and hateful, the wiry gunman already had it in for the tall man. He just wanted to try the drifter, to face Slocum in a head-on fight. Slocum could see it in his countenance, the grimace of a killer.

Rattman pointed a finger at him. "Me and you. We's gonna tangle."

Slocum nodded, pulling the brim of his hat low over his eyes. "After the trail drive," he said in a low voice. "No need to mess up this business we're in. Is there?"

A strange smile stretched over Rattman's thin lips. "Okay, if that's what you want."

Slocum pointed backward. "Now, go ride drag, Rattman. And keep whistlin' if you see strays."

That pissed him off. Slocum was almost enjoying it. Rattman's face turned bright red.

"Go on," Slocum urged.

"This may not wait till the end of the drive," Rattman said through gritted teeth.

"I got nothin' agin' you," Slocum replied. "You have it like you want it. Just don't 'spect me to be afraid of you, Rattman. 'Cause I'm not. You call the tune—fists or pistols. Then we'll see who pays the piper."

Rattman turned and galloped away.

As soon as he had left, Garrity rode up next to Slocum. "He givin' you a hard time?"

Slocum stared straight ahead. "Some men just can't help themselves, Garrity."

"I reckon. He's all mouth, anyway."

Slocum wasn't so sure of that. Rattman had to be able to shoot. With a temper like his, somebody had probably drawn on him. Rattman was still alive, so that meant he could take care of himself.

Garrity gazed up at the sky. "Gonna be a hot one. Think we oughta keep 'em movin'?"

"When's the last time they had water?" Slocum asked.

"Two days ago."

The tall man from Georgia shifted in his saddle. "They should be good today. We might see the San Simon tomorrow mornin', but if we keep 'em movin', we might lose some in the dark. Stop tonight, ride at dawn. That should put us at the river tomorrow afternoon, maybe earlier."

Garrity rubbed his chin, nodding his approval. "Think so? That's good. Real good. Once we hit the San Simon, how much do we have to go?"

"Three days at the most," Slocum replied.

"Couldn't ask for much better, John. Glad to have you along."

Slocum just wanted to get the drive over with, to fill his pockets with some more of Garrity's gold. He could get his pay and skedaddle before Rattman caused any real trouble. Forty dollars and a rifle—one of the best jobs Slocum had seen in a while. And Slocum figured it would be finished in a hurry.

At dark, they stopped the herd. Slocum knew they weren't close enough to the river for the cows to smell the water. The steers settled into a large, docile circle. There had to be a thousand head. And all of them were branded with symbols common to Mexico.

Slocum tagged Rattman and Shorty for the first night watch. Neither one of them liked it, but they stayed with the herd, anyway. Bill and Cal made a fire, heating cans of beans on the coals. They offered a plate to Slocum, who ate it all down. But when the two boys tried to pull the tall man into an after-dinner conversation, Slocum excused himself and rode out to be alone.

He wouldn't need a fire on this warm night; just a bedroll and his saddle. His body ached after a day of riding herd. Maybe he was getting too old to be a cowboy. He made camp and smoked a hand-rolled cigarette.

"John!" The echo reverberated through the night.

Slocum sat up on his bedroll, peering into the darkness. Garrity called him again. Slocum called back.

The high-hatted man rode up to him. "What you doin' out here, John?"

"Just sleepin' some. Figger to relieve Rattman in a few hours. Then the greenhorns can take the last watch."

Garrity chortled. "Yeah, they are kinda green. I offered 'em both a shot of whiskey and they plumb turned it down."

Slocum licked his lips. "Whiskey?"

"The good kind," Garrity replied. "From Kentucky. You game?"

Slocum nodded. Garrity tossed him the bottle of red-eye. It was good whiskey. Hardly any burn or aftertaste. Slocum took one small swallow.

Garrity laughed. "Hell, you can do better than that. Take another."

Slocum swallowed more deeply. The liquor almost brought a smile to the tall man's face. He had fallen in with good company, even if Garrity was running stolen cows to sell to the U.S. Army.

Slocum gave him back the bottle. Garrity took another slug himself. He started in about how much he hated this trail drive, at least until he sensed that Slocum wasn't in the mood to talk.

"Well, reckon I'll leave you to your forty winks. See you in the mornin'." He turned the gray and rode off.

Slocum fought the urge to like Garrity. He wasn't sure he could trust the round-faced man, even if Garrity had put the fate of the herd in Slocum's hands. There was still no good reason for Slocum to relax. He slept fitfully until an unexpected visitor arrived in the middle of the night.

At first the tall man thought a rattlesnake had crawled in beside him. He felt the wriggling shape. It roused him from his sleep. Sweat broke over his face as soon as he opened his eyes. Then he smelled her, sweet and tempting. No rattler smelled like that.

He sat up quickly. "Rosita!"

The girl rubbed her eyes. She had been sleeping next to him. Where the hell had she come from?

"I follow you," she told him.

He asked her how.

She pointed to a small burro that was tied next to the gelding. Her family had given her the animal. She said she was following Slocum all the way to Santa Fe. He told her he wasn't going to Santa Fe, but to Pima.

Rosita stared blankly at him. "Are Mexicans een Peema?"

He shook his head, telling her that she could not go along. A trail drive was no place for a woman—especially with a rough customer like Rattman running around. Not to mention the fact that they were riding into Apache country in a couple of days.

"Go to Fort Bowie," he told her. "You can get a stage to Santa Fe or maybe Tucson."

Rosita had her own answers for the tall man. She put her hand on his crotch. Slocum felt his response to her hand. He stiffened through his jeans, causing her to smile.

"Kees me, Slocum."

He frowned at her. "You remember my name."

Her dress rustled as she pulled it over her thighs. "Slocum."

She guided his fingers to her wetness. He touched her as she fumbled with the buttons of his fly. As soon as she had freed his manhood, Slocum rolled over on top of her.

Rosita spread her legs, guiding him in. They squirmed on the bedroll, raising a little dust. Slocum collapsed on top of her, climaxing, feeling her as she trembled beneath him.

He rolled off and leaned back against the saddle. "You can't come with us, Rosita. It isn't safe for you."

She snuggled into his chest, ignoring him. In a few minutes she was snoring away. Slocum stroked her hair before he got up. He had to relieve the night riders. He saddled the chestnut and tied his bedroll in place.

Rosita protested when she realized that he was leaving.

Slocum told her he had to ride night herd. He also warned her to go back to Dos Cabezas or some other town.

Rosita cursed him in Spanish, telling him that she could survive just fine on her own.

Slocum shook his head but he hesitated before turning the chestnut away. "These cows. What do you know about 'em?"

But Rosita only spat at him. She continued cursing in Spanish. He had made her angry and she wasn't going to tell him a thing.

He guided the gelding away from her, heading back toward the herd. He didn't feel right with the woman there. It would surely lead to trouble sooner or later—although Rosita had followed the trail drive without them seeing her. Maybe he should just forget about Rosita and let her take care of herself. He hadn't asked her to come along.

He finally found Rattman and Shorty in the dark.

"'Bout time!" the thin-lipped pistolero said.

"Yeah," Shorty rejoined. "We been out here all night."

Rattman hit his partner in the chest. "Shut up, Shorty."

Slocum nodded toward the camp where the boys were sleeping. "Get some shut-eye."

"You askin' or tellin'?" Rattman replied.

Slocum urged the gelding forward, moving away from them. "Suit yourself. You don't want to sleep, that's your business."

He could hear Rattman grunting behind him. Slocum just let it roll off his back. He had seen punks before, hotheads who liked to play with guns. Those kind didn't last long. A man had to keep his wits if he was going to survive west of the Mississippi. If you went looking for somebody to kill you, it probably wouldn't take much to find him.

He rode on around the edge of the herd. Slocum had never minded riding night herd. It was peaceful, quiet, untroublesome. Even the wildest dogie would settle in after the sun went down.

Slocum listened to the lonely howl of the coyotes in the distance. A few of them might sneak in to look for a loose calf. But they weren't any real threat to the herd. At worst, a coyote or even a puma would only kill one steer. And most animals would run the other way as soon as they detected the man-scent on the breeze.

A few hours before day, Slocum rode into the camp, waking Bill and Cal for the last shift. Rattman and Shorty were asleep. Garrity rolled over in his blanket and gaped up at Slocum.

"Everythin' all right?" Garrity asked.

Slocum nodded and told him that they were just changing the watch. The herd was fine. They'd be moving out soon.

Garrity climbed back under the blanket and began to snore.

Slocum rode away, leaving the younger men to watch the herd. He wanted to find Rosita, to convince her to go. But when he finally found his resting place, the girl and her burro were no longer there.

5

By the afternoon of the next day, the cattle could smell the river. They lifted their noses to the air, seeking the water to quench their thirst. The herd began to move more quickly. Thick dust rose in a cloud over the plain.

Garrity rode up next to Slocum. "What is it?"

The tall man nodded toward the trail ahead. "The San Simon. They know where it is now."

Garrity frowned and tipped back his Stetson. Sweat poured from his chubby face. He wiped his forehead with the back of his hand.

Slocum wasn't the kind to offer comfort, but at ten dollars a day he figured he could give his opinion. "They'll be okay, Garrity. Let 'em go."

"Sure we won't lose any?"

"They'll stop at the river," Slocum assured him.

The dust billowed as the steers broke into a dead run.

Garrity continued to sweat until the mud ran down his cheeks. Slocum held steady, watching as the other men circled in to meet them.

"What got into the herd?" Shorty asked.

"Smelled the water," Garrity replied. "Leastways that's what John said." He gestured toward Slocum.

Rattman chortled, shaking his head. "Ol' John there seems to know all there is 'bout punchin' cows."

The two younger men looked nervous. Their eyes fell on Slocum, like they were afraid he might make a move on Rattman. But the lanky son of Dixie stared straight ahead, tall in the saddle of the chestnut.

They lost sight of the herd for a while, but like Slocum had said, the river held every steer better than barbed wire.

The San Simon flowed shallow and sandy, a narrow ribbon through the arid plain. When Bill and Cal saw the water, they whopped and drove for the flowing stream. Garrity nodded to Slocum, but the tall man did not return his smile. It hadn't really taken much to figure that the herd would stop to drink.

Shorty gaped at the river, a buck-toothed expression of awe. "Gawsh, Rat, he was right."

Rattman spat into the dust. "Dumb luck."

Slocum spurred the chestnut and broke into a run for the river.

The younger men were already bathing in one of the deeper pools. Most of the steers were in hoof-deep water, sucking in liquid through their muzzles. Slocum dismounted and stuck his face into the river. He drank slowly to avoid the cramps that could come on a hot day.

They all enjoyed the water, bathing and washing out their dirty clothes. When Garrity sought Slocum's advice, the green-eyed rebel told him they should wait until morning to move. The herd should have a chance to drink before they started up again. They'd be easier to manage with full bellies. With the brush around the river, they'd also have a chance to graze, to fatten up.

Garrity went along with that reasoning. Things were going fine so far. Hiring Slocum, he said, was the smartest move he had made.

Rattman scoffed at the compliment.

Garrity eyed the gunman. "What the devil is your truck with this man, Rattman? You mind tellin' me? John hasn't done anythin' to you."

Rattman glared at Slocum, his eyes narrow. "He just looks like a shit-eater to me. Ain't you a shit-eater, John?"

Slocum was pulling on his shirt, which had dried rapidly in the sun. He ignored Rattman's slight. Then the black-eyed gunslinger made a mistake. He reached out to put his hand on Slocum.

"Hey, rebel, didn't you hear—"

Slocum wheeled with a roundhouse right, slamming Rattman in the temple. The hateful man went down into the damp sand along the riverbank. They weren't wearing their guns because they had just come out of the water. Rattman scuttled toward his holster, which hung dry on his saddle horn. Slocum knew he would never reach his own Colt before Rattman drew down on him.

But then Rattman seemed to stumble. He teetered for a few steps and fell face first into the sand. He looked back at Garrity, who had tripped him. Rattman snarled and started to get up again.

Garrity drew his sidearm. Bill and Cal also went for their guns. Shorty hesitated with his hand on the butt of an old Army Colt.

Rattman gaped at Garrity. "What—"

"Hold still, Rat," the chubby man rejoined. "You got no call to start up with John. Not while there's business."

"He's right," Bill said. "I'm with the new man. Rattman, you ain't caused nothin' but trouble since you signed on."

Cal nodded in agreement. "That's right. And you ain't much of a cattleman, neither."

Garrity looked at Shorty. "You figger'n' on tryin' somethin'?"

Shorty locked eyes with his partner. Rattman shook his head. Shorty backed off, raising his hands.

Rattman softened some. He wasn't used to looking into the one-eyed stare of a pistol bore. Rattman had figured that his compañeros would side with him. Only they had taken up arms on behalf of Slocum.

Garrity frowned at Rattman. "Look here, Rat, are you in on this or not?"

A smile from the sheepish gunman. "Sorry, Garrity. I—just—well, I been nervous-like. I don't know, it's just—well, I feel like we're bein' followed. I felt it since we left Dos Cabezas."

Slocum wondered if Rattman had caught sight of the girl. He had seen no reason to tell the others about Rosita. What if they found her themselves? They might hurt her and Slocum couldn't abide that.

Garrity wiped the sweat away from his upper lip. He glanced nervously toward the north. It would be dark soon. And they were getting closer to Apache country.

Bill and Cal seemed to catch the jitters. They studied the glowing highlands to the north. It made them forget about Rattman.

"Aw, there's no danger," Garrity said. "The army's got men out here. They're gonna meet us in Pima."

Rattman shook his head. "Apaches ain't afraid of soldiers. They'll take us when they want us."

"Yeah," Shorty echoed. "When they want us."

"Circle around in back of us," Rattman went on. "Come right up behind you and whack your scalp off before you know it."

Bill looked at his friend. "Cal, you never said nothin' about Indians."

Garrity waved it off. "Aw, there won't be any trouble from the Apaches. Hell, we're takin' 'em their beef. They won't mess with us."

But Rattman had them. Slocum almost admired the way he had turned it around. Even the devil could be persuasive sometimes.

Rattman glared straight at the tall man. "What you got to say about it, reb? Any Injuns hereabouts?"

Slocum just looked away and said, "Don't get too far from your rifles." ·

He saw the change in Rattman's face. Slocum had out-bluffed him. Now maybe the man would keep his mouth shut.

•   •   •

Just as he had done on the previous night, Slocum split away from the others. He didn't have to station them on night herd. With all the talk of Apaches, nobody was going to sleep much.

Mounted on the chestnut, the tall man took a wide swing around the herd. He was looking for Rosita, praying that she had left for parts unknown. He didn't like to think what would happen to her if scum like Rattman got hold of her. But she was nowhere to be seen.

Slocum finally gave up and made his camp in some rocks by the river. He placed the Winchester next to him on the bedroll. Slocum had earned the rifle and the ten-dollar gold piece. He had done all right since he ran into Garrity. Although, on this particular night, the man in the ten-gallon hat didn't come to share his whiskey. Probably saving it all for himself, Slocum thought, to ward off the case of the jitters.

It wasn't likely they'd run into Apaches until they got north of Pima, near the new reservation. And since Slocum didn't plan to go any farther than Pima, he figured there wasn't much risk.

Leaning back on the saddle, he tried to close his eyes. He listened to the sounds of the night, which were a lot louder than a man might expect. Plenty of creatures came to life after the sun went down, even on an arid stretch of the Arizona Territory.

Slocum finally managed to sleep, waking to the sound of falling pebbles in the night. He sat up, levering the rifle, half-expecting an ambush from Rattman, but it was only Rosita, arriving again from the darkness.

"Why're you hol'in' a rifle at me?" the girl said to him.

Slocum lowered the barrel of his new Winchester. "For once, I'm glad you came."

"You won' tell me to go?"

Slocum shook his head. "Not right now. Sit down. I want to talk to you. I got some questions."

He figured there were a few things the girl could clear up. She knew more than he did and she had been trying to tell him all along. Now Slocum wanted to pick her brain, put everything in line, just so he'd know where he was going.

Rosita sat down next to him. "Food?"

She had fry bread and some beans. Slocum filled his belly. The meal tasted of hot peppers. He wondered when she had found time to cook.

Rosita put her hand on his face. "You don' stink, cowboy. You have a bath in the reever?"

He pushed her hand away. "You been wantin' to talk, woman, so go ahead and tell me."

She looked away. "Wha' talk?"

He turned her face toward him. "Miguel. Garrity. The one named Rattman. You know about 'em?"

She nodded.

"And they're together?"

Again her pretty head bobbed up and down.

Slocum sighed. He had nothing against the alliance, especially since Garrity and the others had taken his side against Rattman. He still wanted to know exactly where he stood, even if it meant walking away from ten dollars a day. With the rifle and the gold piece he was ahead of the game. And he had worked his two days.

"Tell me about Miguel and Garrity," he said to the woman.

She sighed and lowered her head. "Miguel. He steals the cows."

"Who from?"

Rosita shook her head. "Fra' all. My people. He takes an' sells to Garrity."

"Steals from his own people?"

"Why I leave heem," the girl replied. "Eet was no right."

The tall man from Georgia gazed out into the darkness. "Tough territory. If you can't hold on to it, there's plenty who'll come to take it from you. Funny thing is, a man never knows when he'll have to face his own reckonin'. Pay for what he's done."

She scoffed at him. "Miguel weel never pay. He's fat niño. Baby. Cry at hees mother's breast."

Slocum hadn't finished with her. "All right. So Garrity buys the cows. What? Dollar a head?"

She made a slashing motion.

"Half that?"

Rosita nodded.

Slocum did the figuring in his head. A thousand head at

four bits made five hundred dollars. The last time he had taken notice of such things, beef had been going for at least three dollars a head. Slocum was willing to bet that the army could be talked into paying five dollars a steer, especially since they were in a hurry to get the beef to the reservation.

Garrity planned to make between three and five thousand dollars on the herd. No wonder he could afford to pay Slocum ten dollars a day. Fifty Yankee dollars was nothing from such a huge ante.

Rosita slid next to him. "I mees you, Slocum."

He touched her hair. "You oughta go, Rosita."

"No."

"Then be careful. I think Rattman mighta spotted you today. What you know about him, anyway?"

She told him that Rattman was a hired gun brought in from New Mexico. Some said that he had been a regulator in one of the land wars. Rosita had never seen him kill anyone, but Miguel spoke of his reputation.

He asked her about Bill and Cal. They were just wranglers, she replied, because Garrity needed someone to help him with the herd. He was only paying them three dollars a day. Rattman was getting ten, same as Slocum, and Shorty wasn't paid anything. He just tagged along with Rattman.

Rosita didn't know much about Garrity. Miguel had met him in Tucson. She wasn't sure if Garrity had concocted the scheme, but she did say that the round-faced man had been the one to make contact with the army. Garrity had made the arrangements to sell the cows and get them to Pima.

So that was how it stood, Slocum thought. A couple of enterprising men had found a way to make a lot of money. And who would say anything to them if they were caught with a bunch of Mexican cows? Garrity could always say he had bought the steers from Miguel. He probably had a bill of sale to back up his claim.

As for the Mexican end of things, there wasn't much law past Nogales and what was there could be easily bribed to look the other way. The only ones who really got hurt were the little people whose cows were stolen in the first place. Slocum felt bad about profiting from their loss, but he had to face the facts. *He* had not rustled the herd and he needed the money. His refusal to help Garrity wouldn't bring the cattle back to the Mexican ranchers. A man had to look out for himself; otherwise he'd starve to death.

Rosita leaned against his chest.

Slocum patted her gently. "I can't help you, honey. You oughta go now, before you get hurt."

"Peema," she said. "Mexicans een Peema?"

"Maybe."

"Men?"

He nodded. She was pretty enough to attract all kinds of men, though Slocum doubted she'd ever settle with one who'd do her any good. He leaned back on his saddle. Rosita stretched out next to him.

"How the devil do you follow us?" Slocum asked.

"You slow," she replied. "An' the dust. You can no see me."

He almost laughed. Five grown men had shown their fears about Indians, and here was this young woman, riding a burro in their wake. Rosita didn't seem to be scared of anything. The girl began to snore on his chest.

Slocum closed his eyes, drifting off.

When he woke again, the girl was on top of him. She had freed his cock from his jeans. Slocum felt her wetness as she guided him in. Rosita moved until they were both finished.

She rolled off, rising, heading for her burro.

"Where you goin'?" Slocum asked.

She shrugged. "To the dust. Where you can no see me."

Slocum had given up. The girl had a will of her own. If she killed herself in her wanderings, he could not be held responsible.

Leaning back on the saddle, he closed his weary eyes, half wishing for a shot of whiskey to ease his aching bones.

Slocum slept for a while, waking in a few hours to see Rattman standing over him in the first light of daybreak.

"I coulda killed you in your sleep," said the black-eyed outlaw. "But I didn't. When it happens, it'll be face to face. I'll give you a fair chance, reb. But you're still gonna pay."

Before he could reply, somebody hollered out. It sounded like Garrity. The chubby man was calling for Slocum. And from the tone of his voice, Slocum knew that something had gone wrong.

6

Garrity stood with his back to the river. Shorty and the two boys were beside him. They were all looking down at the ground, hovering over a bulky brown shape.

Slocum hurried toward them, looking down at the same unfortunate sight. Garrity wiped sweat from his forehead. The morning was cool but he was soaked from perspiration.

Rattman came up beside Slocum, glancing at the ground. "What—? My God."

Garrity exhaled, tipping back the ten-gallon brim. "Found it just now. Dead as a doornail."

Slocum studied the fallen steer. Its tongue lolled out to one side. The eyes were still open.

Shorty's weasel face gawked at the animal. "You sure it's dead?"

Slocum touched the hide. The steer was still warm, which

meant that it had died less than an hour ago. But what the hell had killed it?

Garrity glanced at Slocum. "He dead, John?"

Slocum nodded. "But not long. Better check for Apache arrows. Just to make sure."

They had to roll the animal over on its other side. Rattman and Shorty didn't help. They just stood there, watching.

Slocum and Garrity searched, but they couldn't find any sign that the steer had been killed by Indians, which made Slocum feel better. If an Apache had killed a steer so close to their camp, it would have meant that the Apaches were set on a game of cat and mouse, tormenting the trail drive until the final attack. On the other hand, if the Apaches had wanted to take a steer for food, food that they were going to get anyway, then the cowboys never would have seen them coming. They'd just take what they wanted and disappear quietly into the hills.

"I don't like this one bit," Rattman said.

Garrity looked at Slocum again. "John?"

Slocum told them his theories about the Indians. It made sense to Garrity and the others, even though Rattman continued to snarl. Some men refused to listen to reason, which resulted in conflict most of the time.

Bill laughed a little, his tender face breaking into a nervous smile. "Hell, dead cow ain't no big deal on a trail drive. It happens all the time."

Cal nodded in agreement. "Sure; they just give out, drop dead on the spot. No big deal."

Garrity sighed, looking down at the carcass. "Well, I reckon we shouldn't let it go to waste. Anybody know how to dress out a cow?"

Bill and Cal had cleaned a steer before. Both of them had thick, broad, razor-sharp skinning knives. They showed the impressive steel blades to Garrity.

The chubby man told them to go ahead and take the best parts, leave the rest for the buzzards. The two younger men stropped their blades on boot leather. They seemed to be relishing the task.

Rattman moved around in front of the dead steer. "Well, I'm going to make sure it's dead."

He drew his pistol, a Remington .44, and blasted two

holes in the head of the animal. Then he spun the .44 on his finger before he flipped it into his holster. He turned to glare at Slocum, as if to challenge him.

The tall man from Georgia shook his head. "Pretty good at shootin' a dead cow, Rattman."

"Why you—"

His hand moved for the .44 again.

Slocum dropped his hand as well, bringing up the Colt .36. He beat Rattman to the punch. The black-eyed gunslinger had only managed to get the Remington halfway out of the holster.

Everyone froze, waiting for Slocum to shoot Rattman. It would have been a fair fight. Rattman had gone for his gun first. No jury or judge would have convicted Slocum for the shooting. It was a clear case of self-defense.

Garrity's nervous eyes flicked back and forth between them. He wasn't sure Slocum would pull the trigger. Rattman deserved whatever he got. He had been pushing for it.

Behind Garrity, Shorty went for his gun. Bill and Cal jumped for the little man, grabbing him before he could get his pistol out of the holster. They wrestled him to the ground, pinning him.

Slocum held steady with the Colt. He didn't really want to shoot Rattman, even if it did seem like a good idea. If he let Rattman live, the ornery gunman would surely try again. Slocum knew there was only one way to stop it.

He thumbed back the hammer of the Colt. Rattman's eyes grew wide as Slocum drew a bead between the outlaw's eyes. He figured the end was coming so he had nothing to lose by drawing the .44.

As soon as he started to lift the Remington again, Slocum dropped the barrel of the .36 and fired one shot at Rattman's gun hand. The slug ripped through flesh and bone. Rattman screamed, lifting the hand as blood began to flow.

The Colt smoked in Slocum's hand. It had been the only way to put Rattman out of commission without actually killing him. Gunplay was the one thing a man like Rattman understood.

Garrity glared at the man who danced around his bloody hand. "You satisfied, Rattman? Huh?"

Rattman just kept screaming. Garrity took his Remington, leaving him without a pistol.

Slocum holstered the Colt. He didn't feel good about shooting the man. But he didn't feel badly either.

Garrity drew closer to the tall man. "Yes or no, John. Can we take these cows to Pima without those two? The four of us, I mean. You, me, and the kids there."

Bill and Cal were still holding down Shorty. They peered toward Garrity and Slocum, like they wanted to know what they should do next. Slocum figured they could take the herd to Pima without Rattman and Shorty. Hell, the two of them hadn't been much help. And the herd would be easy to push along the river. The cattle wouldn't stray far from the water. He told Garrity as much.

The chubby man turned back to Rattman, who still screeched in pain. "That's it, Rat. You're gone."

Garrity threw a sack of money into the dust. "There's your day wage since you signed on. Don't let me see you 'round this herd no more."

Bill and Cal asked what to do with Shorty. Garrity told them to take his gun and let him up. The little man scampered to his feet, seething like a cat-cornered rodent.

Garrity shook his head. "Well, I can't give you back your guns, not now. Bill, get their mounts. Cal, you help him hitch 'em up."

Shorty made a move toward Garrity.

The chubby man was quicker than he looked. From nowhere, his hand produced a thick-bore derringer.

Shorty gaped at the pistol. He didn't want to die.

"Try me, short stuff," Garrity said to the mousy man. "I don't have a conscience like this rebel here. I'll drop you like a fry-biscuit in hot grease."

Shorty backed off. "Don't want no trouble, Garrity."

Bill and Cal came back with two mounts. Garrity took their pistols and stuffed them into the saddlebags of Rattman's pinto. Then he led the horses away from the herd, slapping them on the hindquarters. Both animals broke into a run, galloping away across the plain.

Garrity gestured toward the retreating horses. "Better get movin', boys. Won't take long to find 'em. Prob'ly a day or two. The rest of us better mount up and get started."

Bill pointed to the dead steer. "What about that, Mr. Garrity?"

"Aw, take what you can in a couple of minutes. We'll roast it after dark. Head 'em up."

Bill and Cal went to work on the animal, carving out the meat.

Slocum kept his green eyes on Rattman and Shorty. The smaller man had led the wounded gunfighter down to the river. They were washing the blood from his hand.

When he was satisfied that the pair was no longer a threat, Slocum returned to his campsite. He saddled the chestnut, readying himself for the day's ride. The drive would be easier now that they had the river to follow. It wouldn't matter if they were short two men.

The lanky son of Dixie swung into the saddle. He gazed out over the herd, which seemed to be calm. Bill and Cal were draping chunks of meat over their saddles. Garrity came galloping back toward Slocum.

He reined up beside the chestnut. "Too bad about that trouble with those two. I guess some men don't even know why they got so much hate in them."

Slocum nodded toward the herd. "Better get 'em movin'. I'll ride drag now."

There wouldn't be too much dust along the river. Slocum could see strays from the rear of the herd. Garrity should ride point, the tall man said, to keep an eye out for the soldiers.

"You said we were s'posed to run into the army out here," Slocum said.

Garrity exhaled. "That's what I was told. Should see 'em in Pima."

Slocum felt all right about their chances. It couldn't be more than a two- or three-day walk to Pima. The small town was barely a bump on the vast Arizona plain, but it would be a welcome sight to the cowboys.

Garrity left for the point.

Slocum guided the chestnut toward the rear of the herd. He had to cut back some strays, but for the most part, the animals were as docile as newborn calves. Slocum's single gunshot had not spooked them at all.

When he was behind the herd, he began to whistle and

shout, swinging a rope in a circle, urging on the reluctant dogies. Slowly the herd began a northward trek. Bill and Cal swung around on the sides, whooping to make the cattle go forward. Some of the animals didn't want to walk with a bellyful of cool water. But they had to fall in when the mass of cows pressed on.

Slocum rode drag with a bandanna tied around his face. There was some dust to eat. He kept swinging back and forth, cutting back the strays that wanted to lag. Cal dropped off to help him for a while and then he crossed the river to ride the opposite bank. Some of the steers tried to ford so they had to be stopped.

They kept on without incident, driving north into the heat of the afternoon. It wasn't the greatest work a man could get, but Slocum could take pride in getting the job done. He thought about the payoff at the end. With money in his pocket, he'd be set for a while. He could go where he wanted, maybe head to the northwest, into the high forests of Oregon.

His green eyes looked forward, toward the rolling plain. He told himself to think about Indian country, where the drive was heading. Apaches had to be respected, even when they were living on a reservation. However, Slocum saw no signs of Indians, nor did the cavalry appear on the horizon. The herd rolled on without trouble, following the shallow bed of the San Simon. It was almost too easy.

Toward dusk, Garrity circled back and asked Slocum to get the herd settled for the night. The tall man galloped to the front, cutting off the big bull that had been leading them. It didn't take long to get them drinking and foraging by the riverbank.

Slocum looked over his shoulder to see the flames rising from a huge fire. Bill and Cal had already managed to spit-stake the hunks of meat over the flames. Beef for dinner. Slocum spurred the gelding, making for the smell of roasting meat.

Garrity stood by the fire, nursing a bottle of the good Kentucky whiskey. Slocum dismounted but did not cast an overt glance at the liquor. Instead, he took out his tobacco pouch and began to roll a cigarette.

"You got enough there for two?" Garrity asked. "I haven't had a smoke in a while."

Slocum offered him the first hand-roll. Garrity repaid the gesture by giving the tall man a hit from the bottle. Slocum took a generous slug of the red-eye.

Garrity gestured toward the kids. "The boys did a good job on that steer. I'd give 'em a shot of my bourbon if they were a little older."

Slocum hunkered by the fire. The whiskey made him feel warm inside. It eased some of the aches and pains that came with riding herd on a bunch of steers. He finished rolling the second cigarette and lit it from the fire.

Garrity sighed, staring at the flames. "Better keep our eyes peeled for Rat and Shorty. They might get feisty and try to come after us."

Slocum glanced at the chubby man. "Garrity, I think there's somethin' you oughta know."

"I'm listenin', reb."

"I'll punch these cows, help you get 'em to Pima, but I'm not a hired gun like Rattman."

Garrity grimaced. "You seemed to hold your own with him."

Slocum looked at the fire. "He's a fool. Not as fast as he thought. More guts than brains."

"I brought him for his gun."

"I know," Slocum replied, "but if we're lucky, we won't have any trouble between here and Pima."

The chubby man took off his ten-gallon hat and wiped his forehead. "Are you sayin' you won't back me in a fight, John?"

"No. If I ride with you, you can count on my gun. But I won't kill anybody for you, unless they're tryin' to kill me."

Garrity nodded. "Fair enough. By the way, you're makin' twenty dollars a day now. Till we get to Pima."

Slocum accepted the pay raise. No need to be modest, not since they were riding into Indian country. And he knew Garrity could afford to part with the money.

Bill and Cal looked up from their work.

"It's ready, Mr. Garrity," Bill said.

Cal had begun to hack off thick slabs of beef.

They ate until their bellies were full. Cal was a good enough cook to whip up some crude biscuits. He also caught the drippings in a pan so they'd have some sop for the bread.

Garrity became more generous with the whiskey after dinner. Even the two boys had a slug. Slocum took only one more drink. He liked the whiskey glow, but he didn't want to lose his senses. They still had to think about the herd. Like it or not, the green-eyed Georgian was the trail boss.

"Who's on night herd?" Bill asked.

Slocum looked at Garrity, who was now too drunk to ride. "Take the first watch, Bill," he told the young man. "Cal can go next and I'll take the last one. Let Garrity sleep."

Slocum knew he had to get some shut-eye himself. He rode off down the riverbank, retracing a path to the south. He had seen some rocks that would provide shelter in the night. There was a stretch of brush to provide a cushion for his bedroll. He'd have to beat the bushes some to flush out any snakes that might be hiding there.

He made his bedroll and stretched his body on the blanket. As tired as he was, Slocum found that he could not close his eyes. He kept waiting for the girl to appear. Would Rosita come on this night?

He sat up on the blanket. What if Rattman and Shorty found her? They would treat her badly, probably kill her in the end.

No, Rosita was too smart for them. They'd never find her. She'd be able to avoid them on the expanse of the plain. Of course, the girl wouldn't be clever enough to avoid the Apaches if they wanted her.

Slocum leaned back on the bedroll. His head hit the saddle. He peered up at the night sky. He finally managed to sleep, dreaming that Rosita had come to rest beside him. But when he woke, he was alone under the dark sky. He felt sad that he might not see Rosita again. He hoped she had gone off to a better place.

Then he heard the cows bawling and he forgot about her. He had a job to do. He saddled the chestnut, riding out to finish the final watch on night herd.

7

Slocum had the chestnut pointed east, toward the rising sun. The air was clear and cool. Morning birds whirred back and forth as they fed on insects. Slocum knew he had to wake the others, to get the herd moving. But he couldn't pull himself away from the first rays of daybreak, the sliver of orange that peeked over the horizon.

He turned his head south, searching for any signs of movement. But Rosita was not there. Nor did he see the two men who had been fired from the drive. Less determined grudge-bearers had sought revenge when they were thought to be finished. There was no sign of them, however. Not on this morning. It was the kind of start that almost made a man glad to be alive.

Slocum rode back to camp, rousting the two younger men. Garrity groaned in his bedroll. Bill and Cal tried to goad him

51

into action. Slocum waved them off. It would be best to let Garrity sleep until the whiskey had left his head. He wasn't much of a wrangler, anyway.

The boys broke camp and helped Slocum get the herd moving. Again the sated dogies ambled lazily to the north, closer and closer to Indian country.

Slocum thought better of leaving Garrity by himself. When the cattle had passed the campsite, he rode back to wake the chubby man. Garrity slowly came to life, cursing the empty bottle on the ground next to him.

He gawked at Slocum, his face as white as wool. "Kill them two little men for me, pardner."

Slocum squinted at the pale man.

Garrity laughed. "I mean the two men inside my head. One's got a hammer and t'other one's takin' a shit."

The tall man cast his green eyes to the distance. "Gonna be seein' the hills soon. There's forests up there, but I think they're mostly beyond Pima. We got to break from the river, too. But it won't be far from the town. Maybe one of us can ride ahead, scout the direction."

Garrity's eyes grew wider. Thoughts of Apache country were sobering at least. Some Indians didn't want to accept the new way, even if most of them were going along with it. When bucks got their backs up, they would take to devilment or sometimes become outright renegades. Red Buck had been known for devilment most of the time. He hadn't become a full-fledged renegade—not yet anyway.

"I reckon these cows are a peace offerin'," Garrity said.

Slocum figured if their luck held, they wouldn't have to see Red Buck or any other Apache. "Garrity, I want t' get these cows to Pima, draw my pay, and clear out. The sooner the better."

Garrity drew an intrepid breath. "I'm with you on that, Johnny-boy. Let's move 'em out."

Slocum spurred the gelding, heading back to the herd. Bill and Cal had the cattle moving steadily along the riverbed. Slocum sought them out and told them they would have to make the break from the San Simon either that afternoon or the morning of the next day, depending on how much ground they covered. Neither one of the boys had been in

Pima before, so they weren't sure where the break would have to be made. Slocum told them he would scout ahead. He trusted them enough to leave them with the herd.

Bill and Cal smiled at the tall man's compliment. They tried to joke with Slocum, but he didn't bite. His silence impressed upon them the need for serious business on the rest of the drive.

Garrity finally caught up to the herd. He pulled next to Slocum. Sweat poured off him. He didn't look good.

Slocum asked if Garrity knew the trail well enough to spot the break for Pima. The chubby man replied that it was probably marked well enough for them to see it. That made sense to the green-eyed Georgian. There weren't any other settlements up this way, so the trail to Pima was probably well-traveled.

Garrity asked him for another smoke. Slocum stopped to roll a pair of cigarettes. He had to look in his saddlebags to find a dry match. They rode again, smoking as they followed the herd.

Slocum thought of the girl, who had given him the fine North Carolina tobacco. She had probably headed for Tucson, or maybe for Santa Fe. He figured he was still in debt to her. He would probably never get a chance to pay her back. A man couldn't always settle his accounts, even when he wanted to.

"John?"

Slocum glanced toward Garrity.

The chubby man was squinting at him. "You just had the strangest look on your face, pardner. Musta been thinkin' about a woman." Garrity laughed.

Slocum spurred the chestnut and headed after some strays. He cut the animals into the herd again. His voice rose as he whooped and hollered. He still wasn't wild about being a cowboy, but for twenty dollars a day, Slocum figured to give it his best effort.

The riverbank rolled upward into high, steep banks that made it more difficult to follow.

The herd bunched together in a depression that signaled the end of the lowlands. Here the earth began a gradual rise to the forested mountains above Pima. Slocum figured they had to be near the break with the river.

Garrity stared upstream. "Gonna have to turn 'em. Take 'em across. Circle around, maybe."

Slocum decided to scout ahead. Garrity wanted to stay with the herd. He was nipping at another bottle of whiskey, so the hair of the dog would cure him. Slocum could move faster without him.

He rode downstream until he found a place where the chestnut could climb over the bank. When he was on the other side of the San Simon, he raised his hand and waved to the younger men. They seemed to know what he was going to do. They started circling, trying to turn the herd toward the north bank of the river.

Slocum drove the gelding hard until he saw the trail leading north. There was also a sign, declaring that Pima was only twenty miles away. He turned back to rejoin the herd.

Garrity was glad to hear that they were so close. Bill and Cal had already gotten most of the cows into position. Slocum helped them by cutting in the few strays. They decided to keep the cows in the river basin until morning. Then they could drive them northwest at first light. By dusk, they'd be in Pima.

"Army supposed to have put up corrals," Garrity said. "Should be glad to—"

Garrity froze, his mouth wide open. He gaped toward the north. It was still light enough for him to see the sky.

Slocum saw it, too. A thin curl of smoke rose into the air. Smoke from a fire. Could it be a fire in Pima?

Bill and Cal rode in, pointing at the smoke. They asked Slocum if the fire could belong to Apaches. The tall man nodded.

Garrity told the boys to go back to the herd.

They cast one more look toward the smoke and rode away.

"What you think?" Garrity asked.

Slocum sighed, shaking his head. "Things have been good up till now. I was hopin' we had played out our last share of bad luck. Maybe we haven't."

"That fire's too close to be Pima," Garrity offered.

Slocum agreed. But he saw no reason to scout it. If there were Apaches by the fire, no white man would ever catch them. And if the fire didn't belong to Indians, then there was no reason to worry. They didn't have enough men to stand up to a war party of Apaches. Slocum figured if the hostiles came, their best chance was to run and let the Indians have the herd.

"I wouldn't want to be tortured by Apaches," Garrity said. "Mescaleros can make a man pray for death."

Slocum shifted in his saddle. "They're gonna have to catch me first. General Grant couldn't kill me. Red Buck might pick up where Grant left off."

The chubby man shivered, even though the air had warmed. "Red Buck. Don't like the sound of him."

Slocum didn't like it either, but there wasn't much they could do. He watched the smoke curling in the sky. It rose into a stronger current of air that dispersed it into wispy feathers. The feathers hung there until the sun went down and they could no longer see the smoke from the bank of the river.

The night was still around them. Slocum had camped with the others around the fire. They decided to skip the shifts on night herd. It would be better to lose a few cows than to separate the group.

All four of them had their rifles in hand. Garrity cursed himself for firing Rattman and Shorty. He could have used the extra guns.

Slocum sat with his Winchester across his knees, listening to the breeze. The dogies were bawling. They were more skittish than they had been for most of the drive. A few coyote howls rose in the night. Maybe a brave pack was coming close to feed on a lagging steer.

He could have ridden out to chase the coyotes. But that would mean leaving the others. And Apaches made the same howl as a coyote. It was better to stay by the fire.

Bill and Cal had argued that a fire made them an easy target. Slocum convinced them that it didn't matter. If an Apache was going to find you, he'd do it in the dark. He told them to cook their beef and keep their eyes open. Hang onto their rifles, but don't shoot at any shadows.

It was a long night. Nobody slept much. Garrity even stayed away from his bottle, wanting to keep a clear head.

Slocum napped, opening his eyes every time he heard a sound. Once there was a ripple through the herd and the steers called in the dark, but the sound died down and the herd seemed content again.

More night sounds echoed in the breeze. Owls hooted and screeched, their wings luffing overhead. Coyotes lifted their howls in a ghostly chorus across the plain.

Slocum thought that it was a beautiful night if a man could forget his worries. But then something cracked in the darkness and his eyes lifted again. They all kept waiting for the attack from the shadows, but the Apaches didn't come. At least, not in person.

The four of them were glad to see the sun come up. Without much talk, they saw to their business. Slocum and the boys turned the herd toward Pima. They were all anxious for the drive to be over.

Even Garrity was willing to work. He told Slocum he'd go look for some strays. The chubby man was confident as he rode off. A few minutes later he tore back to the herd with his face white and his hands trembling.

"You gotta look," he told Slocum.

The tall man followed Garrity until they reached the dead steer. This animal had not dropped dead on its own. An Apache war lance had been driven straight through its heart.

Slocum tipped back his hat, scanning the horizon with his green eyes. "Somebody was here."

"Apaches!" Garrity cried.

"Maybe. Could be somebody else tryin' to scare us. Maybe Rattman caught up to us."

Garrity's chest heaved. "Who else could it be?"

"You tell me," Slocum challenged.

"What you mean?"

The tall man looked right at him. "These are stolen cows you bought in Mexico, Garrity. Maybe the man they were stolen from is holdin' a grudge."

"Nah. They'd go after Miguel. He's the one who stole 'em. I'm just the middleman."

Slocum took a deep breath. "Well, they don't want us dead. They just want us to know they're here."

"How you figger that?"

"We're still alive," Slocum replied. "If there's a party of Apaches lookin' for trouble, they'd have given it to us by now."

Garrity seemed to breathe easier.

"There's other Apaches besides those on the reservation," Slocum said. "Some bands of Mescaleros will never surrender."

Garrity glanced back toward the herd. "Let's not tell the young ones about this. There's no need for them to know. I'll just say another cow dropped dead."

Slocum turned the chestnut north again. "When we get to Pima, I'm through with this, Garrity. I just want my pay."

"Get us to Pima first. Then worry about your money."

The herd was reluctant to leave the water, but Slocum and the others managed to get them moving. Their nerves settled as they became involved in their jobs. Slocum almost forgot about the war lance. It seemed like some sort of Apache mischief. Maybe Red Buck was just toying with them.

The ground became more uneven as they veered a little to the west. A clear trail led into Pima. Slocum watched for signs of the village on the horizon. It was a small hole-in-the-wall, no place for a decent man to call home, but certainly a town where a trail rider could lay low.

Garrity stayed close to the chestnut. "You see it yet?" he called to Slocum.

The tall man shook his head. He looked back and waved his hand to Bill. The boy came galloping up on a tall roan.

Slocum gestured ahead. "Your horse strong enough to scout?"

Bill nodded.

"Then go see what you can find. But be careful."

Bill spurred the roan, showing no fear.

"Stout lad," Garrity remarked.

Slocum pulled his hat low, hoping that the kid came back alive.

"I'm gettin' worried," Garrity said to Slocum. "He's been gone about an hour."

Slocum leaned forward in the saddle, pointing to the cloud of dust that rose on the plain. "That may be him now."

They finally saw the lone rider coming toward them. It was Bill on the roan. He had a broad smile on his face.

"Pima's up ahead. That way. Can't be more'n five miles."

Slocum exhaled, nodding. "Glad to hear that."

"There's corrals there, too, just like Mr. Garrity said. Must be five or six of them. Built from saplin's. Still got the bark on the wood."

Garrity was suddenly puffed up with pride. "See, I told you we'd make it. No need to worry 'bout that Indian sign now."

Bill frowned. "What Indian sign?"

Slocum waved him off. "Nothin'. It don't matter now. Did you talk to any of the soldiers there?"

Bill frowned. "Funny thing. Ain't no soldiers there at all. I didn't see a single one."

Slocum glanced at the chubby man. "What you know about this, Garrity?"

"I—I don't know. Colonel Nickles said he'd have at least twenty men there to take over when I arrived with the herd."

The tall man leveled his green eyes on the kid. "You sure you didn't see any soldiers?"

"Not a one. But the corrals are there."

Garrity squinted at Slocum. "I'm not sure I like this any more'n you do, John."

It didn't matter about the soldiers. Slocum said they had to take the herd into Pima, to keep their end of the bargain. They could play the rest of the hand as it came.

Maybe some more good cards would fall their way.

8

As the herd drew closer, Pima became more apparent on the horizon. Slocum decided to ride ahead to scout the town. The herd was moving well and the others could handle it for a while. Garrity wanted to come along, but Slocum urged him to stay with the drive. If there was trouble, then Garrity should be in charge of his own cows.

The gelding covered the ground with ease. Slocum saw the steeple of the small adobe mission. It looked abandoned. The stable seemed to be in operation, along with a hole-in-the-wall sundry store. There was no mistaking the army outpost, a tall wooden building that had been locked up tight. Bill had been right on the money. There were no soldiers in Pima. No blue-coated cavalry officers waited for the herd.

He saw the corrals in back of the army outpost: five empty cattle pens. It would take all of them to pen up the thousand head.

Slocum rode back to the herd and found Garrity. "The kid was right. The soldiers're gone."

The worry on Garrity's face seemed genuine. "Wonder where they went? Maybe they're talkin' to Red Buck."

Green eyes fell on the chubby man. He flinched at the piercing stare. Garrity asked Slocum if he had something on his mind.

"My deal is with you," the tall man replied. "When we finish it in Pima, I 'spect to get paid."

"You will, pardner. You sure as hell will."

One by one, they filled the five corrals. Someone had left hay and there were water troughs already in place. The army had been expecting them. The corrals were strong and high enough to hold the steers.

As he worked, Slocum kept Garrity in the corner of his eye. The chubby man had been good about paying so far. There was no way to tell if he might pull something tricky at the end of the job.

Bill and Cal seemed to have the same idea. They kept their eyes on the man in the high hat. What cowboy hadn't been cheated by a crooked pay boss? How many times had they lost their pay after a drunken night, when they had been promised their wages the next day? They'd wake to a headache with the scalawag nowhere in sight.

When the last corral gate was closed, Bill and Cal fell in next to Slocum. They were looking to him to be their leader. Slocum didn't mind if they tagged along. He was planning to look out for himself. The boys had the right to do the same thing.

Garrity came galloping up on his gray. He smiled at them and tipped his hat. The chubby man seemed satisfied with their effort.

"Good job, boys."

Bill and Cal shifted in their saddles, casting woeful looks at Slocum. They wanted him to speak for them, but Slocum figured he wasn't their father. They had to learn to stand on their own.

Garrity nodded to Slocum. "You done right by me, mister. I never forget somethin' like that."

"Then you ain't gonna forget my pay," Slocum said.

Bill and Cal gazed toward Garrity.

"We'd like to draw our wages, too," Bill said.

Cal seemed a little sheepish. "Yeah, that was three a day, wasn't it?"

Garrity's smile disappeared. "I can't believe you boys would press me for your pay—not after all we been through."

Bill and Cal were embarrassed, but Slocum never wavered. He told Garrity that he just wanted what was coming to him. They were in Indian country, after all. Who could blame them for wanting to get out?

Garrity pointed to the rifle that hung on Slocum's saddle. "And didn't I let you earn that Winchester, John? Look here, boys, I haven't been anythin' but straight with you. Now let's ride on into town and I'll see that you get every penny you got comin'. We'll stash our horses, get some grub, and wash off the trail dust."

Bill and Cal looked at Slocum again.

The tall man from Georgia shrugged. "Hell, where would you run out here, anyway? I'd be able to catch you, Garrity."

The chubby man took off his ten-gallon hat. "I don't believe you can think of me like that. Why, I never cheated anybody in my life. I—"

He went on and on, never once mentioning the fact that the cows had been stolen in Mexico. Some poor vaqueros had been cheated out of their livestock. Slocum listened to the banter, thinking that the guilty man was the one who always squealed the loudest.

"He's comin', Mr. John."

Slocum eased out of the tub. He had been soaking for almost an hour. The stableman had let them bathe in the trough behind the livery. Bill and Cal were standing inside the stable, watching the general store. Garrity had been in there most of the afternoon, supposedly getting their pay ready. The chubby man had thrown them five dollars to buy food and liquor.

Slocum knew better than to get drunk. He still wondered if Garrity might be pulling something. When he was dry, Slocum put on his pants and his shirt. Bill stuck his head through the back door of the stable.

"He's almost here, sir."

Maybe Garrity figured they would be drunk enough for him to run out on them. Slocum had a plan of his own. A plan that involved his hand full of money. Garrity owed him fifty dollars, fair and square.

Slocum pulled on his boots and went into the stable. He drew his Colt from the holster that hung on the end of a stall. Then he motioned the boys into the shadows, telling them not to move unless he gave the signal.

Garrity pushed into the stable.

Slocum hung back, watching as the chubby man went straight for his mount. He stepped out of the stall, leveling the Colt at Garrity. The man in the high hat turned at the clicking of the cylinder.

"John, there you—"

He saw Slocum's pistol.

"John, there's no need for that. I—"

Slocum held the bore on him. "You were just gonna ride on out of here, Garrity. You were gonna leave me high and dry."

"No! Don't be foolish. I was going to talk to you before I left. I mean, you're the one hiding in the shadows, not me."

Slocum waved the Colt. "Prove yourself, Garrity. Convince me that you weren't gonna run out on us."

"All right!"

Garrity started to reach into his pockets.

"Slow," the tall man urged.

Slocum had seen that derringer once. He didn't want it pointed at him. And the chubby man was too quick for carelessness.

Garrity didn't pull the derringer, though. Instead, he took three small bundles of something wrapped in scraps of calico cloth. He tossed the largest bundle to Slocum. It felt heavy, like gold.

"I've got pay for the boys, too. Where are they?"

Bill and Cal came out of the shadows.

Garrity sighed dejectedly. "You too? I swear, don't no man trust another nowadays. Here, I put a little bonus in there."

He tossed the younger men their pay. Bill and Cal counted

sixty dollars each. They thanked Garrity and begged his for-giveness.

Slocum wasn't as contrite, but his eyes did open wider when he counted a hundred twenty dollars. "This is too much, Garrity."

"No it isn't. Here, can you read?"

Slocum nodded. Garrity handed him a piece of paper. It was a message from one Colonel Nickles, asking the chubby man to meet him at a place called Apache Wells, just north of Pima, where the forest began. The message went on to explain that the colonel and his troops were chasing Red Buck, that they would post a man at Apache Wells to meet Garrity.

"That's why I gave you all a bonus," the chubby man went on. "I'd like you to stay here a couple of days with the herd. Somebody's gotta fork that hay to those dogies."

Bill and Cal eagerly agreed to stay two more days.

Slocum winced. He really wasn't keen on the idea of stay-ing in Pima. He wanted to get south again. There was plenty of money in his pockets now.

Still, Garrity had a hold on him. He had come across with the gold. Six double eagles looked good in a man's hand. And who was to say there wouldn't be chances to earn more?

Of course, Garrity could have staged the quick pay scheme. He had the coins all bundled up in case they caught him trying to leave town. The chubby man was smarter than he looked.

"You came this far with me, John. How 'bout it?"

Slocum shook his head. "You got a way of persuadin' a man, Garrity. You countin' the two days in this wad of gold?"

Garrity said he thought that was a fair shake.

Slocum looked at the kids. "You in, boys?"

"We said we were," Cal replied.

Bill nodded, a smile on his face.

"Two days," Slocum said blankly. "After that, you're on your own."

Slocum's arms ached from tossing the hay over the corral. He had been using the fork for two days. It was almost time for Garrity to return. Slocum was going to give him until sunset, then the tall man planned to leave Pima.

He stopped for a while, resting on a bale of hay. He rolled a cigarette and looked out over the corral. Except for eating and giving milk, cows were pretty dumb and filthy. He glanced behind him, spotting the two kids who worked like demons. They had never seen so much money in their lives. They were happy to toil for Garrity.

He returned to the pitchfork, tossing more hay to the steers. The army must have used a hundred wagons to get the hay to Pima. No wonder the trail had been worn so well. The saplings for the corrals had probably been brought down from the forests. Somebody really wanted the plan to work.

Slocum finished at the corral and headed back to the stable. He had been sleeping a lot in the past few days. The trail drive had worn him out. It would be a while before he rode herd again. There had to be some kind of work that was better.

He settled in the hayloft and uncorked a jug of corn whiskey he had purchased from the general store. It was thick and tasted of molasses, but it went down easy, chasing the pain and the worry from all the right places.

Slocum took the bundle from his shirt pocket, unwrapping the calico cloth. He looked at the six double eagles, but he couldn't think of anything to spend them on. He couldn't feel good about the end of the trail drive. Too many things had been wrong. The army men were gone, Garrity had left and wasn't back yet, the money had flowed too easily.

Money was always loose when there was a chance of real trouble. Men who weren't afraid to die required steep wages. Garrity had worked awfully hard to keep Slocum next to him. Maybe the worst was yet to come.

Slocum returned the gold to his pocket. He leaned back in the hay, thinking for a while. He would head south at dark. Two days had been his deal with Garrity. And Slocum had stuck to it. He had the right to leave.

The tall man closed his green eyes.

Nothing was going to keep him in Pima. When he had his nap, he was going to head south again, make his way for Mexico. Six double eagles would last a long time once he crossed the border.

He slept until Bill and Cal woke him. They called from

below. They said they wanted to talk to him. It was late afternoon.

Slocum climbed down and joined them in front of the stable.

Bill was the one who wanted to speak. "Mr. John, sir, well, we wanted to tell you that we're gonna stay on, even if Mr. Garrity ain't back tonight. We feel it's the right thing to do."

Slocum said he appreciated their decision, but he was going to stick to the original deal and ride out at dusk.

"We figgered that," Bill replied. "We just wanted to shake your hand and say it's been good workin' with you."

Slocum shook their hands, trying to remember if he had ever been that green. These two boys had a lot to learn. But he had to give them credit for their guts and their honesty.

"General store man has some stew," Cal offered. "Why don't you—"

Slocum just walked away from them. No need to get too friendly. It wasn't in the tall man's nature. He just wanted to eat something and then get the hell out of Pima.

He stood in the loft, watching the sun as it filtered through the cracks in the boards. The light grew dimmer. Finally darkness overtook the stable. Slocum got up off the hay. It was time to leave. The second day had passed and Garrity wasn't back yet. Maybe he wasn't coming back at all. Red Buck might have finished him and the soldiers, too.

He was reaching for his saddle when he heard the door open and close below him. He expected to hear the stable-man moving around, but instead, the place was silent. Slocum froze, reaching for his Colt.

Listening in the darkness, he thought he detected a slow, deliberate movement. Maybe Garrity had sent somebody after him. Then there was Rattman, another man who held a grudge against Slocum.

The intruder bumped into something that tinkled. Then a long silence followed. More movement. He was damned well being stalked.

Slocum turned toward the upper loft door. It opened onto the street. If he could get down, he could come in behind the intruder and surprise the bastard. Who the hell had come after him?

Easing to the wall, he found the latch on the loft door. It opened without too much squeaking. Slocum saw the rope that hung from a pulley. He grabbed the line and lowered himself down the same way that the stableman lowered hay. His boots hit the ground. Slocum hesitated, listening again.

The stable was quiet inside. He opened the door slowly and let himself in. Something bumped in the shadows.

Slocum thumbed the hammer of his pistol. The cylinder made a loud click.

Slocum moved through the dim stable. He was pretty sure the bushwhacker was heading for the loft. Had the man expected to catch Slocum asleep? Maybe one of the younger men had gotten the idea to steal Slocum's gold. He had seen kids that tender turn bad.

His lanky frame slid around a corner. There was noise from under the loft. The intruder seemed to be searching for the ladder.

Slocum had a back shot if he wanted it. But he had never been one to back shoot. Not if there was another way.

The dark figure started up the ladder.

Slocum made his move. He lunged at the shape, grabbing it, pulling the intruder from the ladder. He managed to throw the bushwhacker into a pile of straw. Not a very big man. Small and light.

He put the bore of the Colt in a round face. "Don't move."

"Caramba!" the intruder cried in a high voice. "Get off me, Slocum. You hurt me!"

His eyes grew wide. "You!"

He took the pistol out of Rosita's face. She had to turn up just now. The only person who could delay Slocum's departure from Pima.

9

Rosita sat up in the hay. She brushed back her hair, picking at the bits of straw that had stuck to her. Slocum could smell her perfume over the dank scent of the stable. He slipped his Colt into his holster, thinking that the girl was going to be a temptation.

"You picked a bad time to show up," he told her.

Rosita glowered at him. "Me?"

"Yeah, you. How the hell did you get here, anyway?"

She shrugged. "I follow you. I—"

Someone else moved in the shadows behind Slocum.

The tall man drew his pistol and turned on the stableman.

"Sorry," the stableman said. "I heard a commotion. Come to see what was—"

He saw the girl in the shadows. He struck a match, torching the wick of an oil lamp. When the flame burned a bright orange, the liveryman lifted the lamp so he could get a better look at her.

"You know her?" he asked Slocum.

The green eyes glared back at him. "Yeah, I know her. She's always turnin' up in places she's not s'posed to be."

"Kinda young for you, ain't she?" the man said.

Slocum reached for Rosita, pulling her out of the straw. He guided her past the liveryman, toward the ladder that led to the loft. Rosita laughed at him. She enjoyed mucking up his plans. He told her to climb the ladder if she knew what was good for her.

His tone didn't scare her, but she obeyed. Slocum was right behind her. He tried to ignore her as she sprawled invitingly on the cushion of hay.

Rosita patted the spot next to her. "I ha' been lonesome, Slocum. Seet wi' me."

He shook his head. "Why didn't you go on to Tucson or Sante Fe? Pima is no place for you."

"Slocum—"

"Don't call me that. I'm John, you hear? Nobody in this town knows my last name and I want to keep it that way."

"Wha' town?" Rosita said sarcastically. "More cows than people. I weesh I ha' go to Santa Fe."

"I wish you had, too."

She got up, moving toward him, putting her hands on his broad shoulders. "I mees you, Slo— John."

He pushed her away. "Don't start on me. It won't work this time. I'm leavin' Pima before the night is out. You oughta do the same."

She frowned at him. "Why you leave?"

Slocum told her about the trouble, how they had arrived to find that the army men were gone. The troops were off in the mountains and forests, chasing Red Buck, the Apache who was fast becoming an official renegade. Now Garrity had been gone for two days and Slocum's deal had ended. Pima wasn't any place to be, not so close to Apache country.

Rosita seemed unfazed by the news. In fact, she had seen some Indians while she was trailing the herd on her burro, had watched them kill one of the Mexican steers. She said she wasn't afraid of the Indians. What else could they do besides kill her?

"You'd be surprised what Apaches can do to a woman," Slocum said. "If you ever saw a woman who's been captured by 'em, you wouldn't talk so much through your hat."

"I don' ha' no hat."

"It's just a sayin'."

He started to grab his saddle.

Rosita pressed her body against him. She begged him not to go. Called him a coward. Said he was loco to leave the two boys alone with the herd.

Slocum tried not to listen, but she wouldn't let up. Still, he didn't waver. His responsibility to Garrity had been fulfilled. He hadn't asked to be made trail boss. He hadn't told the girl to follow him to Pima.

He was about to tell her that when he heard someone below.

"You all right up there?" the liveryman asked.

Before Slocum could reply, Rosita looked down from the loft. "I wan' bath. You ha' bath?"

The liveryman smiled like a man who hadn't seen a woman in a long time. "Sure, I got a tub. Want me to heat some water for you?"

Rosita nodded and told him she would be down in a few minutes. Then she turned back to Slocum, remarking that the liveryman was handsome. Slocum ignored her attempts to make him jealous. He was more worried about her losing her life than finding another boyfriend.

"Rosita—"

But she wasn't about to listen to reason. He watched as she climbed down to flirt with the stableman. She told him where to find her burro. He assured her that the animal, and Rosita, could find comfort in his stable. He didn't care if she was Mexican. Squaws were a different story. The stableman said he had never taken to squaws, but Mexicans were fine because they liked to cook. He pointed her toward the wooden tub and then went to find her burro.

Rosita climbed back into the loft. She found Slocum sitting in the straw. She took off her dress and dropped it into the hay.

"You mees me?" she asked.

Slocum exhaled. "Go take your bath."

She told him she needed a blanket to cover her nakedness.

Slocum tossed her the one from his bedroll, warning her not to get it wet. He was leaving before dawn. Nothing would stop him.

Rosita took a couple of steps toward him, like she thought she could convince him to stay. But the livery door creaked and they both heard the braying of her burro. The stableman called to her, saying that he was going to put a kettle on the stove.

"Your new beau is callin' you," Slocum said.

Rosita spat at him and cursed him in Spanish. Then she wrapped the blanket around her shoulders and climbed down the ladder.

When she was gone, Slocum leaned back and reached for his tobacco pouch. He figured to have a smoke to help him think about it.

As much as he wanted to go his own way, he didn't feel right about leaving the girl in Pima. Why the hell had she followed him? Did she really think Slocum was going to be her salvation? Sometimes women were like the snapping turtles he had known in Georgia: Once they got a hold on something, they wouldn't let go until they were dead.

He heard her below, making nice with the stableman. She was splashing in the tub, asking for more hot water. Probably giving the man a peek so he would keep his hopes up.

Slocum couldn't leave her in Pima, not with the Apaches stirring up trouble. A small town with no soldiers could never stand up to a party of armed braves. Maybe that had been Red Buck's intention, to draw out the soldiers and then double back to hit the town. Slocum sure as hell didn't want to be in Pima if Red Buck rode down on it.

He finished the cigarette, stubbing the butt so none of the sparks dropped into the hay.

What if he took the girl with him? It was the right thing to do, even if Rosita had made her own trouble. No woman should be left alone to fend for herself in the wilds of Indian country.

He'd have to travel more slowly with her along. Of course, he could slip away once they were south again. Leave her in Dos Cabezas or some town with a stage stop.

A pretty girl like Rosita belonged in a place where she had a chance to find a good man and settle down.

That was it. He'd have to take her with him. Maybe he could find another horse, trade the burro and some cash for an animal that would be able to keep up the with the gelding. She was sure as hell complicating things. If he left her to her fate, nobody could fault him—except himself.

There was part of Slocum that wouldn't die, the man who had been taught to respect women. A Southerner could never leave a good woman in peril. It would haunt him for the rest of his life—a life that might be considerably shorter if Slocum stayed in Pima.

He heard her below, still flirting with the stableman. Slocum wondered if she would give it up to him. He got his answer when he heard her on the ladder, climbing again to the loft.

Slocum was going to tell her that she was going to leave with him, to head south again, away from Indian country. But when he saw the soft curves of her body, he decided to tell her after they made love.

The glow from the oil lamp shined up into the loft, illuminating Rosita's form. Her long hair was wet and tangled on her shoulders. She moved closer to him, peering down with dark eyes.

"You theenk I'm pretty?"

He nodded.

"Take your clothes off," she said.

Slocum knew he was wasting time. He wanted to be on the trail, heading away from Pima. But he also wanted to lie with her, telling himself that she might be more willing to listen to reason if he touched her.

Rosita shook her wet hair, sprinkling water on him as he started to unbutton his shirt. She told him that she had to comb her hair before they did it. The comb was in her cloth bag.

Slocum watched her as she bent over. Her breasts tilted toward the floor. He felt his heart pumping. Sometimes a man could go a whole year without finding a woman who wouldn't make him pay for it. And here was Rosita, dogging his steps all the way from Dos Cabezas. He wondered how he would end up paying for everything she had given him.

They all made you pay sooner or later.

She continued to fuss with her hair. Slocum removed his boots and his pants. He felt cold in the loft. He got up to retrieve his bedroll blanket. He wanted to spread it on the hay, to make a bed for them.

As he picked up the blanket, Rosita brushed against him. His body caught fire when her soft skin touched his. His desire overtook him. He wanted her in the worst way.

Rosita peered at him with heavy lidded eyes. "Do you love me?"

But he could not talk about love. Instead, he bent to press his lips to her mouth. Rosita kissed him for a moment but then broke away, laughing at him. She wanted to tease, to play. Her giggling resounded through the stable.

Slocum wondered if the liveryman was listening. He had to be careful. Sometimes a meek man got braver when a woman was around. He didn't give a damn. He wanted her now, underneath him, squirming as they both found their pleasure.

He spread the blanket over the straw. Rosita tossed her hair around her head between strokes of the comb. Slocum reclined on the blanket, waiting for her. He hoped he could find the patience to make her come to him. He didn't like showing his weakness for her.

Rosita stood there, gazing at him. "You wan' me, Slocum?"

"I told you not to call me that."

"You wan' me, cowboy?"

"Yeah, I do."

She moved slowly, as if she wanted him to ache a little more. She told him that she loved him, though he knew that neither one of them believed it. When she stretched out next to him, he did not touch her right away. His green eyes took her in, as if he was seeing her for the first time.

"Rosita—"

"Wha'?"

"You're—you're just pretty, that's all."

"Kees me."

Their lips met. Suddenly she wasn't so coy. They wrestled on the blanket, their arms wrapped around each other.

Slocum touched her dark thighs. Her legs parted. His hand found her wetness. Rosita moaned when he touched her.

"Slow," she told him. "No fast."

He kissed her brown nipples which were firm and erect. When he started to draw away, she pulled him back to her breast.

Slocum nursed like a baby, his tongue darting back and forth over her nipples. Rosita began to tremble. She pulled his head up, pressing her mouth to his, probing with her tongue.

His hand traced the curves of her torso. The wetness flowed between the pink labia. She flinched when his fingers touched the top of her cunt. She spread her legs and pulled at him, trying to get him to mount.

Slocum figured it was his turn to tease her. He guided her hand to his erection, telling her that he wasn't ready yet. Rosita didn't waste any time in priming him. Her head dipped between his legs. She took his cock between her thick lips.

Her head bobbed up and down. A shiver ran down the length of Slocum's body. His legs suddenly felt weak. He grabbed her shoulders and put her on the blanket.

"No more play," he said softly.

Rosita was ready. She spread her legs for him. Slocum rolled on top of her, prodding the entrance of her cunt. When she shifted, arching her back, he slipped in.

Rosita cried out.

Slocum started to move.

Rosita met each thrust with a motion of her own, bucking like a fresh bronco.

It didn't take them long to reach their climaxes.

Rosita held him there inside her. She didn't want him to pull out. Slocum put his head on her bosom, trying to find his breath.

"I love you, Slocum," she said.

That made him roll off her.

"Slocum—"

He looked at her, his brow fretted. He told her to stop calling him by his last name. He said that love didn't matter. If the Apaches came, they would both be sorry. Rosita had to see the seriousness of the situation.

But her eyes closed and she said she was tired.

Slocum shook his head, leaning back again. Rosita put her head on his chest. She draped an arm over him. In a few minutes, she was snoring away. He knew it must have been rough for her on the trail, but he tried to put a rein on his sympathies. There were more serious matters at hand. They had to get out of Pima.

Even in the loft, Slocum could hear the sound of the cows bawling in the night. The trail drive had paid off, but now it was time to look for some other kind of work. With the gold in his pocket, he had the luxury of taking his time. Maybe California wasn't such a bad idea, even though it would mean crossing a long stretch of desert.

Rosita made a sweet noise. She opened her eyes for a moment and then drifted off. Slocum decided it wouldn't hurt if they both slept for a while.

He dreamed of the war, as he often did. Only this time, Rosita was there with him, calling his name. It was bright and hot and she wouldn't stop saying his name: "Slocum, Slocum, Slocum."

The tall man sat up in the loft.

"John?"

Had he really heard Garrity's voice?

The loft was warm. Bright light spilled in through the cracks in the wooden planks. Rosita was still there beside him. Daybreak had come and gone.

"John? Are you up there?"

It sure as hell sounded like Garrity. The man in the high hat had come back to Pima.

Slocum knew he had slept too long.

"John?"

Slocum wondered how badly he would have to pay for his mistake.

10

Garrity's rising voice woke Rosita. She sat up next to Slocum, opening her mouth. Slocum put a hand over her lips. He leaned close and told her not to make a sound.

"John? You up there?"

Slocum figured he had to deal with Garrity. He reached for his pants, slipping them over his legs. He didn't want the chubby man to know about the girl. There was no telling how Garrity would treat her.

The stableman's voice rose up in the stable. "Find him, Mr. Garrity?"

"No. You say he's in the loft?"

"Yeah, he went up there with the girl."

Slocum flinched. Garrity knew. Why the hell did Rosita have to follow him to Pima?

"I'm goin' up," Garrity said. "He must be here, his chestnut is in the stall. Wait a minute. Did you say a girl?"

Before the stableman could reply, Slocum stuck his head over the edge of the loft. He saw Garrity's big white hat. The chubby man's eyes turned upward to look at him.

"There you are, John. I was afraid you left."

Slocum frowned at his former boss. "Be right down, Garrity."

A smile from the corpulent man. "Hear you found some company."

"I said, I'll be right down."

Garrity held up his hands. "Fine by me, pardner. Meet you at the general store."

"I'm clearin' out today," Slocum replied.

Garrity's jowls went slack. "Y'are? Hey, Johnny-boy, hear me out before you go. I'll buy you breakfast at the general store. The storekeeper said he'd break out a bottle of Irish whiskey."

"I'm not hungry."

"John, I've put some money in your pocket. You've done a good job for me and I've been fair. I even got rid of Rattman 'cause he was doggin' you. Least you can do is hear me out. Don't cost you nothin' to listen."

Slocum figured he should be decent to the man. Garrity hadn't been a bad boss. And he *had* been responsible for filling the tall man's pockets with double eagles.

"All right, Garrity. You can bend my ear. But then I'm clearin' out."

"Good enough, John. See you at the store."

When Slocum turned away, he saw Rosita behind him. She had the blanket pulled up over her breasts. Her eyes were worried.

When she started to speak, Slocum waved his hand. They listened as Garrity went outside with the stableman. Then Slocum sat down next to her, to pull his boots on.

Rosita kept her voice low. "Garrity, he knows me. He saw me an' Miguel. He wou' tell where I am."

"We got bigger worries'n that, honey."

"Wha'?"

"Gettin' out of Pima, for one."

She leaned against him.

Slocum patted her on the shoulder and told her to lay low until he got back. Her hand gripped his forearm. He felt her fear. It was much like his own. He told her not to worry, that they would head south as soon as he gave Garrity the brush-off.

The man in the high hat was waiting for him. A table had been spread with fresh eggs, smoked meat, biscuits, gravy, grits, potatoes, and hot coffee. Garrity had already begun to eat heartily. When Slocum walked into the general store, the chubby man gestured to an empty seat on the other side of the table.

"Sit down, Slocum."

He hesitated, his green eyes fixed on Garrity's hands. "Where'd you get that name?"

"Stableman," Garrity replied. "Said the girl calls you that. Say, where'd you run into her?"

"She just turned up." To cause trouble, Slocum added to himself. She had let his name slip. Now Garrity knew who he was. It didn't matter that much, not since he was leaving.

Slocum sat down, reaching for the fried eggs. He spooned three of them onto his plate. Then he heaped the smoked meat, grits, and potatoes on top of the eggs. Gravy covered the heap.

Garrity smiled. "You eat like a hungry Southerner, Slocum. Y'know, I hail from Texas. We struck a few licks for the Confederacy."

Slocum started to eat.

"Yeah, I fought myself," Garrity went on. "Mostly I ran supplies. Reckon that's what I'm still doin'. I tell ya, sometimes it hurts to deal with these bluebellies, but a fellow has to stay where the tree's ripe."

Slocum ignored him, thinking that he should take some food to Rosita. She had fed him well. When he got her south, that debt would be repaid. No more responsibility to the crazy Mexican girl. He was damned sure amazed at her tenacity, her grit.

Garrity tried to keep the conversation going. "So look here, Slocum, I went north and met that colonel. They think they got Red Buck on the run, so they're gonna stay up there another week to look for him. In the meantime, they want us to push these cows north."

Slocum hesitated, the fork halfway between his mouth and the plate. "I can't do it, Garrity."

The smile disappeared from the chubby face. "You got to, Slocum. I can't take that herd north into Apache country, not me and those two boys."

"The army isn't obliged to spare a few men?"

Garrity's voice was almost a whine. "Naw, they got to stop Red Buck. He's the key to this thing. And they're gonna get 'im. See, if Red Buck's out of the way, they can turn these cows over to the tribal elders. Then the Injuns'll be calm-like. You see what I'm sayin'?"

Slocum dropped his fork and pushed away from the table. "What if they don't catch Red Buck? What if we get caught in a narrow pass and the renegade war party gets the drop on us?"

"Those soldiers are already up there to protect us," Garrity insisted.

"Yeah? How many strong?"

"Twenty-five, thirty maybe."

Slocum shook his head. "Bad odds, Garrity."

"They say Red Buck has half that many braves followin' him. The soldiers outnumber him two to one."

"Fine," Slocum said, "if they're chasin' him on flat ground. But that's Apache country up there, not soldier country. Injuns know the lay of their land like you know your whiskey bottle."

"The U.S. Cavalry—"

"Is just fine on the plain. But if you put 'em in the mountains, those horses won't do any good. You put a soldier and an Injun against each other in Apache country, the soldier isn't comin' back."

Garrity frowned at the tall man, ready to play his trump card. He had wanted to deal with the lanky Georgian in a straightforward manner. Now it was time to get dirty.

He leaned back, staring at Slocum. "How's Rosita?"

Slocum flinched. "It ain't her."

"The stableman described her to a tee," Garrity replied. "It has to be her. How'd she get this far north?"

"Garrity—"

"Miguel will want to know that I saw her. Won't he?"

The chubby man was a whole lot smarter than he looked.

Slocum wasn't going to bite. "I don't care. It isn't my business. If he comes after her, I won't stop him. She's prob'ly better off with him, anyway. Even if he is a rustler."

Garrity seemed to soften a little. "Look here, Slocum, I'm not tryin' to twist your arm. You know I'll pay you good. Hell, you been right there for me every step we took. I never woulda made it this far with Rattman and those two kids."

Slocum leaned toward the chubby man. "I'm not denyin' you been fair with me. But it's only a job to me. And a man can draw his time and leave a job when he wants. It isn't a crime."

"Look here, Slocum. It's not much. Just drive the herd up toward the Salt River. We'll run into the soldiers by then. They can take over."

"You've been sayin' that since we started, Garrity. Only here I am, gettin' closer to Apache country and there still aren't any soldiers. You claim you saw this colonel, but I haven't seen him."

Garrity's eyes narrowed. "Let's talk turkey, Slocum. Forget the Indians. Forget the risk. Any job has risk. A miner's hole can cave in on him. A farmer can get kicked in the head by his plow mule. Cowboy falls off his horse, gets trampled by the herd. If your time is up, you can't escape it."

"Make your point, Garrity."

"Money," the chubby man went on. "That's why a man works. For pay. He gives effort for gold. You give me a good effort, Slocum, I give you gold. Five hundred dollars. Take it or leave it."

Slocum wished that the offer had not sounded so good. Twenty-five double eagles would keep a man alive for a long time. How often did the tall son of Dixie get a chance to make that much money in one lump sum?

"I got the money, too," Garrity said.

"I don't doubt that."

"Five hundred, Slocum. What do you say?"

Slocum picked up his fork again. "Let me think on it while I finish breakfast. You mind?"

"Go on. I'll see if I can find some whiskey."

Slocum tried to come up with reasons to refuse Garrity's generous offer, but he found that he suddenly wasn't so cautious about going into Indian country. Hell, the soldiers were already up there, if Garrity had told the truth.

He watched the chubby man from the corner of his eye. Garrity was waiting for the storekeeper to bring the bottle. The whole thing hinged on Slocum's willingness to trust Garrity. The high-hatted man had shelled out the geetus so far. Five hundred dollars. It sounded better and better.

Garrity came back to the table with the bottle. "How about a snort?"

Slocum shook his head. "No thanks. Too early. I could use some biscuits and smoked meat for the girl."

"Look here," the chubby man said, "I won't say anythin' to Miguel about you and the girl. It's none of my business. But I got to look after my own interests, Slocum. I need your help."

Slocum lifted the coffee cup to his mouth. He drained the dark, lukewarm brew that tasted like tree bark. He still wasn't sure about the deal.

"Garrity, I got to think some more. When are you plannin' to leave with the herd?"

"Depends on you, sir. If you won't help me, I got to find somebody who will. You go north with the herd, I'll leave tomorrow mornin'."

Slocum pushed back from the table. "You'll hear from me by dark."

"That so?"

"You got my word," the tall man replied.

Garrity said that was good enough for him.

Rosita was waiting when Slocum got back to the loft. He gave her the biscuits and meat. She ate heartily, lifting her dark eyes to thank him.

"Garrity knows it's you," the tall man said.

Rosita hesitated. "Miguel—"

"No, he's not worried about that. He just wants me to go along when he takes the herd farther north."

Rosita frowned. "Apache country."

Slocum nodded. "You can't follow me if I go."

"I wouldn't," she replied. "Don' go, Slocum."

She made sense until he thought about the five hundred dollars. How long would twenty-five double eagles free him from the rigors of day labor? With that much money, Slocum wouldn't have to dig another outhouse for a while. He wouldn't have to shovel shit or pitch hay. And Garrity had been right about one thing—any job had some risks.

"Slocum, no!" She could see it in his face.

He turned away, reaching into his pocket for the pouch of tobacco that Rosita had filled for him. He had enough leaf for one more cigarette. The smoke might help him think.

Rosita went to him, putting her hands on his shoulders. "I don' wan' you to die, Slocum."

He wondered if his life was even worth five hundred dollars.

"Slocum—"

"Leave me be, woman."

"I love you."

He drew away from her, climbing down the ladder. He had to be alone for a while. It was the only way to make his decision.

As he came into the street, he saw Bill and Cal going into the general store. Garrity wouldn't have any trouble talking them into the job. They were young and ready for adventure.

Slocum walked around behind the stable. He sat on an empty buckboard wagon and gazed across the sunlit plain. It was going to be a hot day. The drive into Apache country wouldn't be easy. He'd earn every dollar Garrity would pay him.

He considered just riding out, heading south again, leaving all of them behind. Forget about the girl, forget about Garrity. Run for parts unknown.

But what would he be running to? Not much. And he'd be walking away from a chance to earn a fortune.

Slocum sat there for a long time, thinking. He reclined on the buckboard, falling into a light doze. When he woke up, the girl was there beside him, holding his hand.

She looked very pretty in the light of late afternoon.

"Don' go, Slocum," she said softly.

He sat up. His body felt rested. His head was clear. It would soon be time to give Garrity his answer.

"Slocum—"

He put his fingers on her lips. "It's my decision, Rosita. We're not married, so you can't tell me what to do."

"Slocum, por favor—"

She stopped. Her eyes grew wide. She nodded to the man who moved around the side of the stable.

Slocum turned to see Garrity. The chubby man tipped his hat and said hello to Rosita. Her dark eyes looked away.

Garrity's brow fretted a little. "Lookin' for an answer, Slocum. What's it gonna be?"

"Five hundred?" the tall man said.

Garrity nodded.

Slocum sighed. "Half now, half when the drive is over?"

"Fair enough."

"Okay, Garrity. You got yourself a deal."

The chubby man began to count out the double eagles.

Rosita put her hands on Slocum's shoulders. "No—"

"Hush, woman."

The gold changed hands. Garrity told Slocum that they'd be pulling out first thing after daybreak. Slocum said that would suit him. He wanted to get it over with.

Garrity tipped his hat again to Rosita before he left.

"I don' like him," the girl said.

Slocum put two double eagles in her hand. "Rosita, get the hell out of here. Find the closest stage stop and hurry on to Santa Fe. You hear me?"

She nodded, saying that she would leave in the morning, after the trail drive started north.

That night, Slocum brought dinner for them from the general store. They ate quietly. Rosita was sad, at least until they started to make love. She fell asleep in Slocum's arms, snoring like a baby.

He kissed her forehead, closing his eyes.

Five hundred dollars. Half of the money was already in his pocket.

He slept easy for most of the night, waking only when the trouble started just before daybreak.

11

A bumping noise roused Slocum from his sleep. His listened in the predawn darkness, wondering if the stableman had risen early. He heard the soft whinny of a horse. It seemed to be coming from outside.

Slocum figured he had better have a look, even if it was only Garrity coming to wake him. He slipped away from Rosita, who rolled over without opening her eyes. He put on his pants and moved toward the loft door. It had been latched to keep out the cool night air.

The tall man listened closely, waiting for Garrity to call him. Instead, he detected the low hiss of whispering voices. There seemed to be two of them outside the stable. Maybe Garrity had sent the boys to wake him. Or maybe it was some kind of ambush.

Slocum reached for the latch on the loft door. He opened

it a little. The hinges creaked. He tried to look out at the two men below.

But one of them saw him. "There!"

Pistols exploded in the darkness. Lead slugs tore through the planks of the loft door. The splinters hit Slocum in the face. He dived away from the gunfire, landing belly first on the floor of the loft.

Rosita sat up and started to scream.

Slocum crawled to her, putting his hand over her mouth. She clung tightly to him. When she started to say something, Slocum shook his head. He wanted to be able to hear them, to anticipate what they were going to do.

The whiny voice rose in the cool air. "He's up there, Rat!"

Slocum's lip curled as he said the name. "Rattman. That son of a bitch. Rosita, get under the straw. Cover yourself. Don't come out till I tell you. You hear me?"

She didn't have to be told twice. Rosita burrowed into the straw like a scared barn mouse. Slocum covered her with the blanket and threw more straw on top of her. When the girl was out of harm's way, Slocum turned back to the loft door. He crawled even with the portal and listened again.

They weren't going to run now that they knew where he was. Surely Garrity and the others had heard the shooting. They'd come to help Slocum if he just waited.

The door creaked below him. Rattman wanted his revenge. Slocum wondered if he had any more men besides Shorty. The tall man opened the loft door again.

Shorty stood in front of the stable, holding the reins of their mounts. It had taken them a while to catch up with the herd, but here they were. Slocum had to wonder if Rattman had recovered the use of his gun hand, the one that Slocum had put a bullet through. Maybe he was just as good a shot with his other hand.

Slocum heard Rattman moving downstairs. He decided he had to lead them away from the stable. He didn't want Rosita catching a stray bullet.

He stood up, taking a deep breath. The rope still hung in place on the pulley outside the loft. Slocum figured it was his best chance. He stepped quickly in the darkness to find his Colt. Five cylinders were full. He wanted to take Shorty with a single shot, if possible.

Rattman bumped into something downstairs. "It's me, rebel. I come back to git you. Pay you back for what you done to me."

Slocum reached for his Winchester. He jacked a cartridge into the chamber. Maybe he could take Rattman inside, before the gunman got off another shot.

The tall man leaned over the edge of the loft, peering into the deep shadows below him. He could feel Rattman there. The man's breathing rose in the stable. Slocum took aim with the Winchester.

One clear shot was all he needed. Rattman's boots scuffed on the floor. Slocum squeezed the trigger of the rifle. The hammer fell with a harmless click.

Slocum levered the Winchester again, but the firing pin was not working. And Rattman heard the click. He fired into the loft, making Slocum drop the rifle. He had to run for the upper door, hit the planks, leap into the night, catch hold of the rope, and swing to the ground.

Shorty's gun streamed fire in the cool air. He tried to shoot Slocum as the tall man flew from above, but the pistol shots whizzed over Slocum's head, missing him by several feet.

Slocum hit the ground with his Colt in hand. He fired one shot at Shorty, who had emptied his weapon. The slug caught the small man in the middle of the chest. He screamed, twisting around in a circle, calling for Rattman to help him.

"I'm hit, Rat. I'm—"

He slumped to the earth with his last dying breath.

Slocum broke into a run, heading for the general store. Garrity was sleeping there, in back of the place. The boys were close by, camping next to the corrals. If Rattman hadn't brought any more guns with him, they'd have him outnumbered four to one.

The shooting had awakened Garrity. He was up with his Colt .45 in hand. He drew a bead on Slocum as the tall man approached.

"It's me, Garrity."

The chubby man lowered the .45. "What the devil's goin' on?"

"Rattman."

More movement to Slocum's right. He and Garrity pointed their pistols at the shadows. Bill and Cal stopped dead in their tracks.

"Mr. Garrity, we heard shootin'."

"Rattman came back to get Slocum," the chubby man replied. "Get your rifles, boys. We're gonna take care of this once and for all."

They hurried back to their bedrolls to get their Winchesters.

Garrity eased to the back corner of the general store, peering toward the stable. "He got Shorty with him?"

"Not anymore," Slocum replied.

"That son of a biscuit-eater. He won't rest till he gets himself plumb killed."

Slocum figured that statement to be the truth.

Garrity glanced back at him. "The girl. Is she in that stable?"

The tall man nodded. "I hid her pretty good."

Bill and Cal came running up behind them.

"Ready, Mr. Garrity."

"We're loaded for bear."

Garrity looked at the stable again. "I wonder if the stableman is still in there?"

"Would you be there?" Slocum asked.

"I see your point. Okay, how 'bout this? We fan out, come in on all sides. Give him a chance to surrender."

"He won't," Slocum said.

Garrity looked at the boys. "You're prob'ly right. Boys, you two hang back. Me and Slocum'll go in."

Slocum shook his head. "All three of you stay back to cover me. I'll take him. It's me he came after."

"That's all well and good," Garrity replied, "but he's messin' up my business, too. I may not be much at punchin' cows, but I can shoot."

Slocum looked at the sky. "Whatever we do, it better be quick. The sun'll be up soon."

"We could wait him out," Bill offered.

Slocum's green eyes fell on the livery. "The girl is in there."

Garrity didn't seem to care. "We got to finish this, Slocum. Boys, you two get under the porch of the general store. When we flush him out, you take any shot you can get."

Bill and Cal moved to their posts.

Garrity turned to Slocum. "How you wanna do it?"

"You cover me. I'll try to get around to the back."

Garrity rubbed his chin. "Better get my rifle. Where's yours?"

"That firin' pin broke," Slocum replied. "You were right. I should have taken it to a gunsmith. Only there isn't one out this way."

"Wait here," Garrity said.

The chubby man moved into the back of the store, coming out with his Winchester in hand. "I'm gonna put one right between his eyes."

A window opened above them. The storekeeper looked down to ask what was wrong.

Garrity warned him to go back to bed, stay low, not to come out until he was told.

The window slammed shut.

Garrity took a deep breath. "Let's go get him."

They started to move in the shadows.

Slocum wondered if Rattman had found the girl yet. Maybe he wouldn't see her under the hay. He had more important things to worry about.

They stopped about halfway, crouching in the darkness. Slocum gestured to the right, toward the side door of the livery. Garrity nodded.

The tall man started to move.

Garrity also rose up. Then the rifle barked from the loft. A stream of fire erupted through the swinging door. Garrity buckled, falling to the ground, holding his right arm.

Immediately, the two younger men opened up with their rifles.

Slocum looked back at them, screaming for them to stop. Rosita was up there. She might be hit with a bullet.

The boys let up.

Slocum crawled back to Garrity, who was still alive.

"Got me in the wing," the chubby man said.

Slocum began to drag Garrity back toward the general store.

The rifle exploded from the loft.

Again the two kids raised their weapons, returning fire on Rattman, driving him back.

Slocum managed to pull the chubby man to the porch of the general store. Garrity groaned as the blood poured from his arm. Slocum told the boys to take care of him, to stop the bleeding.

Bill had a scared expression on his tender face. "But Rattman—"

"He's mine," Slocum replied. "I've got to get him before he finds the girl. If he—"

But it was too late. They all heard the scream. Rosita cried out in the stable. Rattman had her.

"What we gonna do now?" Bill asked.

Slocum didn't have the slightest notion.

"Rebel!"

The cry resounded in the darkness.

"I'm comin' out, you green-eyed bastard!"

Bill and Cal cocked their rifles.

"No," Slocum said. "Wait for him."

They held their breaths, watching the stable for signs of movement.

Rosita cried out again.

Slocum grabbed Cal's rifle, raising it to his shoulder.

Rattman came out of the barn with Rosita in front of him. She was naked. Rattman fired off one shot at the general store, causing them to dive for cover.

"I want the reb!" Rattman cried.

Slocum looked over the edge of the porch. "You got me, Rattman. Just let the girl go."

Rosita screamed for them to kill Rattman.

The outlaw put a hand over her mouth. "I'm gonna kill her, rebel! If she—"

Rattman cried out in pain. Rosita had sunk her teeth into the hand that Slocum had wounded before. The gunman relaxed his grip on her. Rosita immediately broke away from him, running toward the general store.

Rattman started to take aim on her with his rifle, but Slocum quickly fired a couple of rounds over his head, shooting high so the girl wouldn't be hit. Rattman flinched, afraid of them, now that he didn't have his shield.

The bushwhacker reached for the reins of his mount.

Slocum stood up, trying to get a good angle on him. He fired one shot as Rattman swung into the saddle. The outlaw spurred the animal, driving hard away from Pima.

Slocum and Bill shot at him as he departed, but they missed the moving target in the dark.

Rosita rushed to Slocum, throwing her arms around him.

"Get her a blanket," Slocum said. He wanted to cover her nakedness in front of the others.

Bill offered his coat. Slocum wrapped the girl in it. Her body trembled in the cool air.

"I'm goin' after Rattman," the tall man said.

Garrity moaned. "No, Slocum. You can't."

"Why not?"

Garrity coughed a little. "Get me inside."

The two boys helped him into the general store. They called to the storekeeper who came down with an oil lamp.

"What the hell was that all about?" the proprietor asked.

Slocum waved him off. "Just an old friend from hell, come to call. Get that light over here. And find us some bandages."

Bill and Cal eased Garrity into a chair.

Slocum looked at the boys. "Gonna need your skinnin' knife."

Bill reached into his boot, coming up with the shiny blade.

Slocum cut the sleeve away from Garrity's shirt. He studied the bullet wound. The slug had gone clear through the fleshy part of the bicep. At least they wouldn't have to dig out the lead. The bone didn't seem to be broken.

"How's it look?" Garrity asked weakly.

Slocum exhaled. "I seen worse. Bullet passed through. The wound looks pretty clean, but we've got to seal it."

"Gunpowder," Garrity said. "Just give me a shot of whiskey first."

Slocum broke down a couple of rifle cartridges while Garrity had his snort. Then the chubby man nodded that he was ready. Slocum packed the black powder in the wound. Bill and Cal had to turn when the lanky Georgian struck a match to the powder.

Garrity screamed as the wound sparked and fizzled. When it was over, he asked for more whiskey. Slocum had a shot himself.

Bill shook his head. "You're a brave one, Mr. Garrity."

Cal had to run outside to vomit.

Garrity rolled his eyes at Slocum. "Don't go after Rattman, reb. He's finished. He won't be back."

Rosita echoed the sentiments of the wounded man. "Don' go, Slocum."

Garrity gestured to the girl. "Bill, take her back to the stable. See if the liveryman is all right. And take Cal with you."

Bill nodded, hesitating until Rosita agreed to go with him.

Slocum glared at Garrity. "What's on your mind?"

The wounded man looked toward the storekeeper. "Can you leave us alone for a couple of minutes?"

The man nodded and went upstairs.

Garrity turned his eyes on Slocum. "You got to take this herd north, Slocum. Get it to the army."

"Rattman is—"

"To hell with Rattman. There's money involved here. You think that five hundred I'm payin' you grew on a tree?"

He coughed and then drank from the whiskey bottle.

"The army's gonna pay on delivery," he told Slocum. "That means you got to bring the money back to me. I'm trustin' you. Just bring it back here."

Slocum frowned. "How much money?"

"Five thousand," Garrity replied. "I got a thousand steers at five a head. You got to do it for me, Slocum. You're the only one I can trust."

Garrity's eyes drooped low. He passed out in the chair. Slocum called for the storekeeper to come and tend the wounded man. The bullet hole needed salve and a bandage. At least the bleeding had stopped.

Slocum started for the door.

"Where you goin'?" the proprietor asked.

The tall man just went through the door, onto the porch. He gazed toward the barn, where the stableman waved from the front entrance. At least he hadn't been shot in the fray.

Slocum knew that Garrity was right. Five thousand dollars meant more than settling the business with Rattman. After all, what was Slocum going to do? Give the two hundred fifty dollars back to Garrity?

There wasn't much for him to do but follow through on the trail drive. Take the cows north into Indian country with the two boys to help him. Any way the tall man looked at it, the drive was going to be rough. He just hoped he didn't have to pay for the effort with his life.

12

Slocum took long strides across the dusty ground that had been stained with blood. The stableman stood over the body of Rattman's partner. Slocum had hit him with a heart shot. The dead man gaped up at him. Shorty's eyes were still open.

"Why'd them boys come after you?" the stableman asked.

Slocum just pushed past him without a reply.

"Hey, what am I s'posed to do with this dead man?"

Slocum glanced over his shoulder. "Bury 'im, leave 'im for the buzzards. It don't matter to me."

Slocum went into the livery, where he found Rosita with the two boys. They were being nice to her. Real gentlemen. They turned to face Slocum.

"She's fine, Mr. Slocum."

"Yeah, she's doin' all right."

His green eyes narrowed on Rosita. "That so?"

She had already changed into her dress.

"Slocum!" She ran to him, putting her arms around his waist. The boys looked embarrassed. They turned away as the girl buried her face in Slocum's chest.

The tall man patted her shoulder. "It's over, Rosita."

"I wa' so afrai'!" she replied.

He let her sob for a moment. Then he pushed her gently away from him. Her dark eyes were puffy. Her thick lips trembled a little.

"Rosita, listen to me," Slocum started. "Garrity's gonna need a nurse to help his arm get better. You go stay with 'im, hear?"

"But—"

"Just do it, girl. You can stay at the general store while I'm gone. I'll be back in a couple of days."

"Slocum—"

"Go on."

Rosita left reluctantly. When she saw the dead body, she quickened her pace, running for the store. Slocum watched from the door until she was inside. Then he wheeled toward the younger men.

Bill and Cal seemed no worse for the gunfight, but Slocum knew they were scared inside, because he was just as fearful. A man didn't always show what he was feeling. Slocum figured they were tough enough to help him, but he still had to say what was on his mind.

"You boys comin' north with me?"

They both nodded.

"Could get rough," Slocum said. "No tellin' what the Apaches will do once we get there."

"We're still comin'," Cal said.

Bill nodded in agreement. "Cain't keep us away, Mr. Slocum. We signed on till the end."

"End may come sooner'n you think," Slocum offered.

Bill shifted a little on the balls of his feet. "Well, if it's so bad, why're you stayin' on?"

Slocum heard a number of answers in his own head. He figured it just boiled down to the money and a lack of sense. But he didn't say that to the boys. He told them to saddle up, to get ready to empty the cattle pens. They were taking the heard north as soon as possible.

Bill and Cal hurried out of the stable, avoiding a look at the dead body outside.

Slocum climbed to the loft, gathering his belongings. He knew he still had time to give it up, to ride south by himself. He could leave Garrity, the girl, the herd. But he had made a contract with the man in the high hat, so he had to carry it through. If he lived long enough, he could come out of the damned mess with a lot of money.

He dropped his saddle to the dirt floor below, climbing down behind it. The chestnut gelding was skittish after all the gunplay. It gave Slocum a little trouble as he cinched the saddle. He couldn't blame the animal. The tall man felt a mite skittish himself. He slipped the bridle over its head and then led it outside.

The stableman was going through the pockets of the dead man. He looked up when Slocum came out. Slocum ignored him. He didn't care what the stableman did with the body. Shorty probably wasn't headed for the gates of St. Peter, anyway. He had lived a hellish life and he would no doubt reap the reward on the other side.

"He's got gold on him," the stableman said to Slocum.

"Keep it."

He led the chestnut toward the general store.

Inside, Rosita sat next to Garrity, who still slept in the chair.

"He still alive?" Slocum asked.

The girl nodded, then said: "Don' go, Slocum. Stay wi' me."

He didn't reply. Instead, he knelt next to Garrity, shaking him gently. The chubby man opened his eyes.

"I got to know where to take that herd," Slocum said.

Garrity nodded weakly. "Apache Wells. Due north. Till you reach the forests."

"Will somebody from the army be there to meet us?"

Garrity nodded again and then closed his eyes.

"I sure hope he's right," the tall man muttered under his breath.

Rosita put her hand on his shoulder. She pleaded with him not to go. Slocum stood up and called for the store-keeper. When the man came into the room, Slocum told him to watch out for Garrity and the girl.

"Can't do it for free," the man said.

Slocum sighed. "Nobody's askin' you to. You'll be paid. But if I get back here and find either one of 'em hurt, you're gonna get paid with somethin' besides gold."

"I'll do my best, sir."

Slocum started for the door.

Rosita stopped him. "Slocum!"

He looked over his shoulder. "I gotta go, Rosita."

"I know. One kees."

He nodded. Rosita ran to him. Slocum pressed his lips to hers and then he was gone, striding out of earshot so he could not hear her crying.

He mounted the gelding and guided it around the general store.

Bill and Cal were ready to go. They looked at Slocum, who waved them toward him. They rode up next to the tall man, trying not to show their nervousness.

Slocum peered at the cattle pens. "Y'all get a count on those steers?"

Bill nodded. "Got three hundred in the first two pens, two-twenty there, two hundred one, and one ninety-nine. Twelve hundred and a few odd ones."

"He knows how to count 'em, too," Cal insisted.

Twelve hundred. That was the first good news, Slocum thought. The army had made the deal for a thousand head. The herd was two hundred more. They wouldn't have to be as careful on the trip north. Who would care if a few strays were lost on the drive?

Bill pointed toward the first corral. "I got the bull in there, Mr. Slocum. We oughta open that one first, get the old boy started."

Slocum nodded. He told Bill to get the first corral open. Cal could get the second and third ones. Slocum would take the back pens.

"Get 'em open quick," he told the kids. "Run 'em all together. Get that bull headed north."

They both looked at him.

Slocum frowned. "What is it now?"

"We just wondered who's gonna pay us, sir."

"Yeah, since Mr. Garrity ain't—"

"Garrity won't go anywhere," Slocum replied. "Now

we're wastin' time with this nonsense. Sooner we get these cows north, sooner we come back here to get our pay. You hear me?"

They nodded and rode off to their tasks.

Slocum felt funny about collecting the money for the herd. If the army really came across with five thousand dollars, then Slocum would have to get the cash to Garrity. That meant a nervous trip back, looking over his shoulder for bandits. At least he'd have the youngsters with him, though he figured they might not be worth much, even if they did have guts and backbone. Slocum shook it off, thinking that he should wait until he got the cows to Apache Wells before he started to worry about the trek back.

Bill opened the first gate to let out the old bull. He waved his hat over his head. Cal and Slocum opened the other pens. It took a while to empty the corrals. Some of the cows didn't want to go in the same direction as the herd. The three riders managed to cut them back, to get them headed north behind the bull.

Slocum brought up the rear, letting the boys do the rest.

He looked over his shoulder one last time, peering toward the general store. Rosita stood on the back porch. She waved to him.

Slocum turned around and nudged the gelding along. He wondered if he would ever see Rosita again.

But then a maverick steer broke away from the herd, taking some of the others with him. Slocum quickly went after them to turn them back. He managed to forget everything except the wrangling chores that would occupy him all the way to Apache Wells.

That afternoon, they led the herd into a small depression between two ridges. It was the perfect place to camp for the night. They wouldn't have to worry about riding night herd. There was even a pool of water in the shallow canyon so the dogies could drink.

Bill and Cal made camp on the high ground. They told Slocum they'd cook on the drive. He wasn't one to argue.

The tall man sat in his saddle, peering out over the herd. It had taken Garrity two whole days to ride to Apache Wells and back. But that was one man on a horse. The herd would move a lot slower. It could take twice as long to get there.

He looked south again. The general store was no longer visible. The ground had become too uneven to see any distance. Slocum knew he could ride back to spend the night with Rosita, but he didn't want to leave the boys alone with the herd.

The sun sank low in the sky. Coyotes and night birds began their search for supper.

Slocum leaned forward in his saddle, wondering if any of the sounds of the dark belonged to Apache warriors.

The hollering woke the tall man from Georgia.

He sat up with his gun in hand. One of the boys was calling out from his bedroll. Slocum got up and ran toward him. The noise was coming from Cal, who trembled like a willow leaf in a cyclone.

"I saw a Injun, Mr. Slocum," he said between panting breaths. "He was standin' right over us. When he saw me, he run."

Slocum looked for signs that someone had been there, but he could not find a thing. "You just had a bad dream, boy."

"I tell you, I saw him, Mr. Slocum."

Bill's brow fretted. "Maybe you was dreamin', Cal. How could a Injun get away so quick?"

Slocum knew an Apache was capable of things that no white man could ever understand, but he didn't say it. There was no need to scare them any worse. He told them to break camp. It was almost daylight.

He went back to saddle the gelding, which had been hobbled for the night. What if the kid had seen an Indian? He mounted the chestnut, looking in all directions, trying not to see Apache braves in every morning shadow.

Where the hell was the army? Wasn't that damned colonel supposed to be out here with his men? There didn't seem to be any sign of Indians or cavalry.

He cursed himself for taking the stupid job, even if it would pay five hundred dollars in the end. What good would the money do him if he had a war lance through his gut? He told himself to keep moving. If the Apaches came, he could just give them the herd. Garrity would understand that.

"Mr. Slocum!"

The boys waved to him. They were ready to go. Slocum joined them and started the herd out of the depression, heading north toward Apache Wells.

By late afternoon, they could see the forested slopes on the horizon. Slocum knew there was no turning back. They were deep in Indian country now. If the Apaches attacked them, there wouldn't be much reason to fight. Running seemed to be the only answer.

Still, except for the boy's nightmare, there hadn't been one clue to suggest that the Apaches were interested in them.

Bill dropped back to talk to Slocum. He asked if they were getting close to Apache Wells. Slocum knew from Garrity's directions that the wells were somewhere near the base of the forests. That meant they would be there by the next afternoon at the latest.

"Didn't take so long," Bill offered with a smile.

Slocum's face stayed grim. He told the boy to get back to his duties. Bill tipped his hat and spurred the roan forward.

Slocum broke away from the herd to cut back some strays. He ended up on a high ridge that gave him a good view of the north. The forests weren't as close as they looked, but he was sure they could reach the wells some time during the next day.

Slocum wondered why Garrity had taken two days to get to the wells and back. They were going to make it in three with the herd. Maybe the chubby man had waited for the soldiers to arrive. Slocum wouldn't have minded seeing a dozen blue-coated riders.

Bill called back to him, waving his hat.

Slocum waved his hand, the signal for stopping to bed them down.

Maybe it would be this easy for the rest of the drive. Apache Wells was almost within reach. One more day and it would be over. And if nothing else went wrong, Slocum could get the hell out of Arizona.

"Apache Wells," Bill cried.

Cal began to whoop.

Slocum rode on ahead, to make sure the circles of water were not a mirage. Clear, blue liquid pooled in the low rocks. Natural springs fed the watering holes. It was a good place for the cows to drink.

He turned his eyes to the slopes above. The trees weren't as thick as the woods in Oregon or Washington, but there were plenty of places for Indians to hide. Or soldiers.

Slocum knew that anyone in the hills would be able to see and hear the herd of steers. There was no need to look for the soldiers. They'd find the herd soon enough, if they were anywhere in the area.

He headed back, helping the boys move the cattle closer to the water. By dusk, the herd was quiet and contented. Still, there were no signs of soldiers or Apaches. The hills were dark and silent.

"Those soldiers'll be here soon," Cal offered.

Bill echoed his compañero. "Yeah, they're expectin' us."

Slocum told them to shut up and make camp. He was too short with them. They both frowned, but Slocum didn't care. He wanted them on edge. No need to forget that they were on the edge of the Apache reservation.

Where the hell were those soldiers?

He slept uneasily that night, waking to the cries of the kids. They yelled for him to come see. They told him to hurry.

Slocum ran to them, looking down at the dead steer. It had been killed during the night. An Apache arrow protruded from its neck.

Slocum lifted his green eyes to the hills. "They've seen us."

Cal started to shake and tremble. Slocum grabbed the boy, slapping him across the face. The kid had to sit down.

Bill patted his shoulder. "It's okay, Cal. They ain't gonna hurt us. If they wanted us dead, we'd have our throats cut by now. Ain't that right, Mr. Slocum?"

But the tall son of Dixie did not reply. His green eyes were turned toward the forested slopes to the east. He was watching for signs of movement in the trees, wondering what the Apaches were going to do next.

13

Slocum looked at the two red-faced youngsters. Their eyes were wide. They had never been in Indian country before. Slocum wasn't too crazy about their present location, but the situation had to be dealt with in a manly way. They still had a chance to come out of it alive.

Bill glanced toward the tall man. "What we gonna do, Mr. Slocum?"

"Yeah," Cal rejoined, "what are we gonna do?"

Slocum tipped back his dusty hat. "Depends on how bad we want our money. You boys wanna get paid?"

They both said they did.

"Then we stick it out, keep the herd here, hope like hell the army comes today or tomorrow."

"And if we don't stay?" Cal asked.

Slocum shrugged. "We steer around Pima on the trail back and hope we never run into Garrity again."

Bill looked at his partner. "Cal, didn't Mr. Garrity say somethin' about a drive from Tucson to Sante Fe? Somethin' about shippin' cows by train? That's s'posed to be the new way."

Cal was nervously glancing at the mountains. "I don't know, Billy. Maybe we oughta go. We all got money in our pockets." He looked to Slocum. "What about it, sir?"

Slocum had that glint of larceny in his green eyes. The notion had come on him when he least expected it. A chance to make a fortune for himself. Why couldn't he dip his bread in the gravy with the rest of the thieves? He had done worse in his day.

He nodded toward the bright peaks of the forest. "Somewhere up there is a squad of cavalry, boys. They're gonna give us five thousand dollars for these cows. Split three ways, that's over fifteen hundred apiece."

They both gaped at him. "What about Garrity?" Bill asked.

Slocum's eyes narrowed. "What about him? He's lyin' wounded in Pima. We get past him, head east or west. Get the hell out of Arizona. He won't ever know what happened to us."

"That's stealin'," Cal offered.

Slocum gave a hard gesture toward the herd. "Every one of those cows was stolen by a Mexican who sold 'em to Garrity. Army's givin' 'em to the Apaches cause we stole their land. Only ones not stealin' is the Injuns themselves. 'Cept for Red Buck. God knows what he's up to."

Bill and Cal cast their gaze on the dead steer. Bill asked why the Apaches had killed the steer. Slocum replied that it was pure devilment, to run them off or scare the hell out of them.

"They might kill us," Cal said.

Slocum exhaled. "They might. But they haven't so far. And we can always run if they attack. If we stay, we're puttin' all our cards on the table. We're bettin' they don't want us dead."

The kids wanted a chance to talk it over. They split away, talking in low whispers.

Slocum couldn't blame them if they wanted to leave. They had their lives ahead of them. On the other hand, he was a worn-out trail bum, hoping to cash in big. The young-sters had better chances if they ran.

Slocum looked toward the mountains again. There were two groups of Apaches up this way. All of the Indians weren't renegades like Red Buck. One group, most of the Apaches in fact, wanted to make their peace with the white man. Maybe he could find the friendly members of the tribe, talk sense to them, hand over the cows, and then go find the soldiers so he could collect the gold.

He licked his lips. A fortune was somewhere in these hills. A blue-coated colonel carried a bag of double eagles. What would it hurt to stick Garrity for the money? One thief sticking another.

The boys came back toward him. "Okay," Bill said, "we're gonna stay, Mr. Slocum. Only when we get our share of the gold, we're gonna take it back to Mr. Garrity. You can do what you want with yours."

Cal nodded in agreement.

Slocum said that was fine with him. He told them to mount up. They would have to keep the herd together while they waited for the soldiers.

"What if the Apaches come?" Cal asked.

Slocum did not reply. He went to saddle the chestnut. He didn't want to think about Apaches. He was sure they'd be around soon enough.

When he was back in the saddle again, he rode a circle around the cattle. Bill and Cal did the same. They couldn't help themselves from glancing over their shoulders, check-ing the slopes every few minutes.

The sun rose high overhead, bringing a heat that forced them back into the shadows at midday. They ate beef and drank from the spring. Nobody said a word. They waited out the afternoon in a tense silence.

Slocum started to ride herd again as the sun sank lower. Dusk was coming on too soon, and still there was no sign of Apaches or the cavalry. It would be a long, dark, sleepless night, full of noises that made a man creep closer to the circle of the campfire.

Shadows lengthened over Pima. Rosita stood on the porch of the general store, gazing to the north. Garrity rocked in a chair behind her, his arm in a sling. The whiskey jug sat on his lap. He had drunk all the good stuff and was now enjoying a batch of crude corn squeezings.

"What the hell you lookin' for, woman?"

Rosita folded her arms. "They ha' been gone too long."

Garrity made a scoffing sound. "Slocum's tough. And those Injuns ain't gonna give 'em any trouble. Hell, as soon as they get there, the army will be on 'em."

She turned to face him. "They shou' ha' come back."

"Quit frettin', Rosita. Come over here and sit next to me. I'll take your worries off that trail bum."

"He ees no trail bum!"

She wheeled away from the chubby man, gazing again to the north. Slocum had to return alive. A good man like him would not die in vain.

"I'm gettin' a mite hungry," Garrity said. "Why don't you go on in an' rustle me up some grub?"

Rosita figured it was better than listening to his drunken ramblings. She went into the general store, calling for the storekeeper. He gave her permission to use the kitchen.

Rosita went to work, preparing a meal for Garrity. He wanted her to sleep with him. He had more than hinted at it. Even with his wounded arm, he still wanted her.

But Rosita could not think of any man but Slocum. She knew it was a mistake to love him, but she could not help the way she felt. Sometimes a woman had no reins on her heart.

"Rosita!"

She told him to wait.

Garrity seemed to be impatient. She heard him come through the front door. Heavy boots stomped back to the kitchen.

A hulking form appeared in the doorway.

"I tol' you to—"

Rosita turned to see a swarthy face grinning at her. "Buenos noches, señora. Que pasa?"

Rosita dropped the pan she was holding. "No!"

The man told her in Spanish that he had missed her. He wanted to lie with her, they way they had done in Mexico. Rosita started to run toward the back entrance. His strong hands caught her.

She started to cry out, but he muffled her voice.

He threw her to the floor, lifting her dress. His fingers pawed the soft hair between her legs. He told her that he loved her, cooing hatefully in his native tongue.

Rosita struggled as he climbed on top of her. She felt his member prodding her. She continued to fight even after he had entered her.

He slapped her face and told her to be still or he would kill her.

Tears poured from Rosita's face as he took his pleasure.

When he had finished, he sat up, looking down at her with his dark eyes. "Was it that bad?" he asked.

She had once enjoyed his bed. Then she had left, complaining about his theft of the cattle from the peasants. He knew her people had rejected her, but she could always come back to him.

Rosita sat up. "I hate you, Miguel." She repeated it in Spanish.

He only laughed. She was his again. There was nothing she could do. The cowboy would not save her this time. And if he tried, Miguel would kill him.

"Sunup can't be too far away," Bill offered.

Slocum just grunted and put another piece of wood on the fire. Nobody had been able to sleep. At least they were still alive. No more sign of the Apaches—not yet.

The tall man from Georgia was considering a short trip into the hills to look for the soldiers. They had to be up there. Then why hadn't they heard them? Maybe Red Buck had led them on a wild-goose chase.

Cal stared into the darkness. "They know we're comin'," he said. "Why ain't they here? Why don't they come and get these cows?"

"I'll go have a look after daybreak," Slocum said. "See if I can find any sign of the cavalry."

"Be careful," Bill said.

Slocum watched the east, waiting for the sun. If he could find the soldiers, he might be able to talk them out of the money. That meant the whole five thousand for himself. He could hightail it before the boys caught on. Outrun Garrity, make for the northwest. Sometimes, parts of Oregon reminded the tall Southerner of Georgia.

"Been the longest night of my life," Cal whined.

"Just be glad you lived through it," Slocum said.

The fire crackled, sending sparks into the air. Slocum kept his gaze turned to the east. The glow began at the top of the trees, getting brighter as the sun rose over them.

Slocum stood up, stretching. "I better go—"

Bill scuffled to his feet, peering north. "Listen."

Slocum frowned. "I don't—"

Cal was right beside his partner. "I can hear it, too."

The tall man listened until he heard the horse approaching. A lone horseman was riding straight for their camp. He came from the north, down the trail through a narrow valley.

Slocum pulled his Colt. "Get your rifles, boys."

They hesitated, frozen with fear.

"Go on," Slocum urged.

"Indians," Cal said.

Slocum shook his head. "No Indian'd make this much noise. But get your rifles anyway. No sense takin' chances."

They picked up their Winchesters.

The three of them stood there, watching as the dark shape drew ever closer to their camp.

Cal pointed toward the rider. "It's a soldier."

Slocum saw that the kid was right. A cavalry officer sat in the saddle of a tall chestnut stallion. The kids waved to him, crying out, happy to see that the army had finally arrived.

Slocum's green eyes narrowed as he studied the soldier's approach. Something didn't seem right. The man's head was too loose on his neck. He didn't respond to their calls. He just kept coming.

As he reached their camp, the cavalry officer slumped forward in the saddle. He clung to the stallion's neck. Slocum saw the Apache arrow protruding from the man's back.

"My God!" Cal cried.

Slocum reached for the man, to help him from the saddle.

"Water," the man said in a hoarse whisper.

Slocum laid him on his side. He might live if they got the arrow out in time. He grabbed the canteen, lifting it to the officer's lips.

When the man had drunk, his eyes rolled up toward

Slocum. "Dead," he moaned. "All dead. All but—"

A desperate sound escaped from his lips. He trembled a little and then died with his eyes open. Slocum knew they should bury him, but as it happened, they never got the chance.

Rosita had to cook breakfast for Garrity and Miguel. She could hear them talking at the table. She hated them. She had to find Slocum and get word to him.

"Can you trust thees Slocum?" Miguel asked.

Garrity nodded. "I think so. What the hell are you worried about? You got your money."

"I wan' more," Miguel replied. "A beeger share."

Garrity sighed. "Okay, Miguel. If that's what you want. I ain't in no position to argue. When Slocum comes back, I'll cut you in for another five hundred. How's that sound to you?"

Miguel's lip curled. "Half."

Garrity rubbed his chin. "Think so?"

"I stole the cows. You geeve me half. Partners."

"Okay, Miguel. Half it is."

"And I keel the cowboy!"

Garrity nodded again. "If that's what you want. Slocum don't mean much to me."

Miguel called to the kitchen, telling the girl to bring more coffee. Rosita had tears in her eyes as she served them. She was hoping to get word to Slocum before he returned to Pima. If she could warn the tall, green-eyed Georgian, he might live long enough to save her from the Mexican. She knew Slocum would have to kill Miguel. It was the only way he could free her.

Cal waved his hands in the air. "That sinks it, Bill. I'm leavin'. If the army can't stand up to Red Buck, then we can't, neither."

Bill looked at the tall man. "Whatta you say, Slocum?"

Slocum turned away from the dead soldier. "The kid is right. As soon as we bury this one, I'm headin' south again. You should do the same."

They started to gather up their gear.

Slocum figured he was still ahead of the game. He had the

money in his pocket. He could also take the cavalry officer's mount, maybe sell it along the trail. The trip would only be a bust if Slocum lost his life.

When the chestnut was saddled, Slocum walked back toward the dead man. He broke the Apache arrow, leaving a stub in the soldier's body. The man deserved a decent burial. A quick funeral, a few words said.

But it was too late for that.

"Mr. Slocum!" Bill cried.

Cal started to scream hysterically.

Slocum's eyes lifted to the slopes above.

The Apaches had appeared on the ridges to the north and east. Their silhouettes formed sinister shapes against the bright sky. A war cry echoed over the valley.

Slocum swung into the saddle of the chestnut.

"What do we do now, Mr. Slocum?"

The lanky son of Dixie replied that it was every man for himself.

14

Bill and Cal watched as the Apaches stood motionless above them.

"Mr. Slocum—"

But he was gone, driving hard to the south.

The two younger men were frozen by the sight of so many Indians.

"Cal! Get your saddle."

The boy had begun to cry. "I don't want to die, Billy."

Bill's hands trembled. "They ain't hurt us yet. Maybe—maybe these ain't Red Buck's renegades."

"I don't want to die!"

Bill reached for his saddle. "Do it, Cal. Saddle up. Follow Slocum. It's our only chance."

A cry broke from above them. The Apaches started to run. Bill and Cal hastened in the face of the attack. Their shaking hands didn't help on the cinch of the saddle.

"Billy!"

"Ride, Cal. Just ride!"

Cal's foot hit the stirrup. But as he tried to lift himself into the saddle, the cinch slipped and the saddle turned sideways. The boy fell back to the ground, landing on his spine.

"Billy!"

The other kid hesitated too long. On the slopes, the Apaches stopped, drawing their longbows, sending a hail of arrows on the two greenhorns. Cal screamed when one of the shafts hit his arm. Billy moved to help him. The second barrage of arrowheads rained down on them. Billy took one in the back, tumbling from his horse.

The Apaches ran again, making for the camp.

Bill and Cal were still alive. They braced themselves, drawing their pistols. But they never got off a shot. They didn't even see the Apaches that put the killing arrows in them. The shafts came from nowhere, silent and brutal like the slap of Satan's hand.

Slocum quickly discovered the Apaches to the south. Some of them had rifles. They opened fire as soon as the chestnut started away from the camp. Slocum thought he might make it, at least until the gelding took a slug in the head. The animal went down and Slocum went with it.

He slammed the hard, rocky ground and the air left his lungs. He fought the deep cramp inside him. If he could draw one breath, he might live.

Air came through his windpipe, easing the fire in his chest. He had to get to his feet. Somebody had been wrong about the renegade. Red Buck's troops were more than a dozen strong.

Slocum staggered as he fought for balance. His back and legs hurt, but fear chased most of the pain. Gunshots resounded from behind him. Lead kicked up dust by his feet.

The tall man drew his Colt, firing back. He couldn't even see them. The shots were coming from behind a ridge to the west. Slocum decided to run in the opposite direction.

A trail of slugs followed him, barely missing as he ran out of rifle range. Where the hell did he think he was running?

Even if he made it back to the forests, the area was crawling with Apaches.

He saw the smoke rising from the place where he had camped the night before. The boys hadn't made it out. Slocum stopped dead on the ground. He could still see the rear of the herd. The cattle were a hell of a lot closer than anything else.

Dust rose quickly behind the western ridge. They were coming around on horseback to get him. Slocum broke for the herd, running as fast as his wobbly legs would allow.

His only chance was to hide in the middle of the herd. Even if the braves started to move the cows, Slocum could always stay low in the dust. When night came, he'd have an opportunity to get away.

The dogies spread out as Slocum wedged between them. He fought his way to the center of the herd, squatting, when the cattle had engulfed him. He prayed that the savages hadn't seen him.

Their voices rose up over the bawling of the cattle. The braves on horseback came over the ridge, making for Slocum's dead horse. They'd know the tall man wasn't dead when they couldn't find the body. Slocum cursed himself for staying. The gold had tempted him and now he was paying the price.

The cows moved around him, calling to no one.

Slocum duckwalked between them, trying to keep from getting stepped on.

Savage voices sent guttural cries back and forth. They knew Slocum was still alive. And they hoped to change that in a hurry.

Rosita stared out the kitchen window, watching the ground behind the general store. Miguel had ridden out a few minutes before, heading south. He would not tell Rosita where he was going or how long he would be gone. Garrity was supposed to keep an eye on her, but the chubby man was asleep on the front porch.

The girl thought she saw her opening. If she could get to the stable, she might be able to ride her burro out of Pima. Then she would go north to warn Slocum about Miguel and Garrity.

Easing through the back door, she started walking toward the corner of the building. The general store owner called from the second floor, asking her where she was going. She replied that her cloth bag was in the stable; she needed her herbs and peppers to season the stew the way Miguel liked it. The proprietor did not want to cross Miguel, so he let her go.

Rosita stopped at the front of the store, peering around the corner at Garrity. The older man slept soundly in the chair. Rosita broke into a run, making for the stable.

The liveryman was glad to help her with the burro. She retrieved the rest of her belongings from the loft. She'd have to survive on the trail again, but it was worth it to warn Slocum.

She came down the ladder, hurrying toward the front door. The liveryman had taken the burro outside. Rosita froze when she saw Miguel sitting on his mount next to the burro.

His hateful eyes fell on her. But he did not hurt her. Instead of venting his anger, he told Rosita to get on the burro. Then he rode toward the front porch to wake Garrity.

It didn't take him long to talk the chubby man into leaving. Garrity had to take a couple of shots of whiskey before he mounted his big gray. The pain was great in his wounded arm, but not bad enough to keep him in Pima.

"You sure they're headed this way, Miguel?"

The Mexican nodded and told him to hurry.

The burro was not fast enough, so Rosita had to ride double with Miguel. They were heading southwest, away from Slocum and all his trouble. Rosita would not get to warn the tall man. As the horses galloped over the rolling countryside, the girl wondered if she would ever see the green-eyed drifter again.

The herd started to move. Slocum had to run in a crouch, which was hard on his back and legs. Still, he managed to stay low in the middle of the herd. The braves were taking the cattle through the narrow valley.

As they drew closer to the wooded slopes, Slocum began to make his way through the steers. If he could get into the woods, he would have a better chance of running away. Maybe he could keep them guessing until dark and then get the hell out of the trees.

He broke through the edge of the circle, bursting out to see Apache war paint staring at him from the back of a pinto pony.

The Indian's eyes opened wide. He hadn't expected to see a white man slipping between the cattle. Slocum made a run at the pony, spooking the animal, causing it to rear. The befuddled savage fell from the pony's bare back.

Slocum immediately jumped onto the pinto, digging his spurs into the animal's sides. The pony burst forward, into the heart of the valley. Lead slugs and feathered arrows whizzed over the tall man's head. He fell forward, grabbing the pinto's mane.

He had to get past the herd. It was clear running after that. Maybe he could find a cave or a hole to hide in.

The pinto spooked a little when he tried to cut through the herd. The trail narrowed into a dry bed of rock. Behind him, the Apaches kept firing their rifles, kept stringing their bows.

But he was almost out of range. Just clear the herd. Find a way into the trees. Pray like hell that all of the renegades had come down from the slopes. There had to be at least thirty of them.

The pinto finally passed the old bull that was leading the herd. A war cry rose in front of him. Slocum saw an Apache riding straight for him on a dark pony. He lifted his Colt and fired several quick shots. The warrior tumbled to the rocky ground. There were no more obstacles except the horde of savages that tried to make it through the mass of cattle behind him.

The Indian ponies weren't good as wrangling mounts. Slocum wished the chestnut had not been killed. It had been a steady animal.

But the pony would have to do. It carried him down the narrow valley, where the slopes grew steeper. Slocum's stomach turned over when he saw the wall of rock ahead of him. There was no way out of the valley, which was quickly turning into a ravine. The Apaches were driving the cattle back there to use the place as a natural corral.

The tall man stopped the pony and slid off its shiny back. Nothing to do but climb. If he could make it to the crest of the rise above him, he might be able to get down the other side.

War cries echoed through the hills. The renegades had made it through the herd. Slocum could see them now. Some were on foot, a couple rode ponies.

He started up the slope, making his way in the trees. He figured he probably wouldn't be able to outrun them, but he was sure as hell going to try. He had a head start and fear to bring him strength.

As he climbed higher, the tree trunks became thicker. He found a path. It ran level across the slope. What if it led to the renegade camp?

He could hear them in the trees below. The braves would be faster in the hills. It was their country. What was it he had told Garrity? Put a white man and an Indian in the same territory and the white man would never come back. And Slocum was facing more than one damned redskin.

He climbed again. The slope was steep, but he could hang onto the trees. There seemed to be more light above him. He had almost reached the crest of the rise. Slocum pulled himself onto a short ledge that receded toward the summit of the peak.

The smell hit him first. He turned to look at the carnage. The sight sickened and horrified the tall Georgian. But at the same time, he thought he saw his chance to escape the savages on his tail.

Garrity and Miguel were at the top of the rise, watching the plain. Rosita sat below on Miguel's saddle. She knew she could turn and run, but she would have to spook the other horse in the bargain. Maybe she should take both animals.

Miguel came down before she could make her move. He dragged her off the animal and took her up to where Garrity leaned against the high ground. The chubby man smiled at her.

Rosita looked away, staring out over the plain. She saw the dust rising over the troop of cavalry officers. There were at least a hundred riders, probably from Fort Bowie.

She looked at the grim faces of Miguel and Garrity. Why

were they afraid of the soldiers? Rosita smiled. Garrity did not want to explain how he had bungled the cattle deal. And Miguel would not like to tell them where he got the stolen cows.

Rosita stared back to the north. The cavalry was heading for Pima. The girl felt better about Slocum's chances. If the cavalry couldn't help the tall man, who could?

The dead soldiers had been stacked in a big pile on the mountain. Red Buck and his braves had slaughtered all of them. But Slocum didn't have time to grieve. He could hear the Apaches getting closer.

Quickly, the tall man removed the blue officer's coat from a dead captain. He had once sworn he would never wear the Union colors, but his life was more important than rebel pride. The coat stank of death but he put it on, anyway. If he could lie in among the dead, the Apaches might pass by him.

His eyes stung with the stench of death. He realized all the soldiers had been scalped. How the hell was he going to hide his full head of hair?

He heard the Indians calling below.

Slocum lay down in the pile of bodies, wedging his head under one of the hideous corpses. The smell almost made him pass out. He wanted to lose consciousness—anything to chase that horrible smell.

The Apaches were right on top of him. They moved in all directions. But no one touched him among the corpses. Still, the search lasted almost until dark, forcing Slocum to breathe that ghoulish odor. He had to play possum if he wanted to live.

The shadows began to lengthen around him. Noise from the searching Indians grew fainter. Slocum figured it was time to take a chance. He raised his head a little.

Nothing. No arrows, no gunshots. Had they really been fooled by his ruse? He climbed off the stack of bodies.

Slocum removed the blue coat and threw it into the pile. He wondered if the memory of that smell would ever leave him. He turned, making for the slope. He had to go slowly and quietly now. It might take him all night to get out of the hills.

The tall man hesitated, looking back over his shoulder. If he climbed even higher, he would have a better vantage point to view the lay of the land. He might even be able to see the plain to the south. What if the ridge led to a better path down?

He had to go around the bodies again. The wall of rock behind them had plenty of handholds. Slocum worked his way up, grunting and groaning, feeling the streaks of pain in his arms and legs. He had to stop to rest a few times, but he finally pulled himself onto the crest of the high ground.

The sun had almost disappeared to the west. Slocum peered south. The ridge sloped downward, gradually easing into the rolling plain. It would be a long walk to Pima, but what choice did he have? Maybe he'd run across a stray mount. That wasn't luck to be counted on.

He could not see the herd below him, but he could hear them. There was also a glow from a fire, but it was on the other side of the ravine. The Apaches were there, probably cooking up a side of beef.

Did Red Buck really think he could start up trouble again? The Apaches had been beaten. Thirty renegades might cause trouble, but they weren't going to chase the white man from the Arizona Territory.

Slocum didn't care. He just wanted to get south. He shouldn't have gone against his better judgment in the first place.

As he lowered his eyes on the path of the ridge, something moved behind him. Slocum turned, but he never saw the Indian club that struck him on the side of the head. He fell to the ground, unconscious.

When he woke up, two Apache braves were dragging him by the arms, taking him into what appeared to be the camp of the renegade leader, Red Buck.

15

They dropped Slocum next to the huge bonfire. He could feel the heat on his face. His green eyes peered into the high flames. The half carcass of a steer browned in the fire. Slocum figured he wouldn't exactly be welcome for dinner. Apaches had been known to burn a man at the stake.

A rough pair of hands bound his wrists and ankles behind him. Slocum was still groggy from the blow on the head. He closed his eyes. The fire was too hot on his skin. He tried to wriggle away from the heat. One of the braves kicked him in the gut. Slocum stopped wriggling.

It looked damned bad for the tall man. And he didn't even have the strength or the chance to make a move. He could only keep his eyes closed, hiding in the darkness, passing out again.

The blessed sleep didn't last long. Cold water splashed

Slocum's face. His eyes opened into green slits. There was a brave standing over him. The Apache had a hunk of broiled meat in his hand.

Slocum could smell the steer cooking. All of the Indians were beginning to cut chunks from the side of beef. The brave in front of him dropped a piece of the meat next to Slocum's face.

The tall man felt nauseous. When he didn't take a bite from the meat, the brave kicked him in the side. Slocum opened his mouth, snapping at the hunk of beef like a gila monster after its prey.

The Apache laughed and called the others to come watch him. A circle formed around Slocum. The brave nudged him to force him to eat. Slocum kept trying, but he could not reach the meat in front of him.

One of the Indians barked like a dog.

The others joined in.

Somebody whistled and suddenly there were two Apache dogs there, fighting over the scrap of meat. Slocum tried to roll away from the dogs, but another foot kicked him. He lay there trying to catch his breath.

Why didn't they just kill him and get it over with?

They might torture him for a while. Have some fun. Stake him out over a rattler hole. Make him pray for death.

The renegades seemed to lose interest in him. They moved away toward the fire. The dogs sniffed around him for a few seconds, but then they were gone. Slocum closed his eyes.

Red Buck had more men than had been reported. There must have been fifty of them, or at least it sounded like fifty Apaches. The renegades had gotten rid of the cavalry without much trouble. Slocum wondered how far the renegades would get before a whole regiment of soldiers found them. Fifty braves with bows and rifles were no match for a regiment. It was little consolation, knowing that they'd get caught someday, that they'd pay for all their murders, including Slocum's death. Damned little consolation.

They lifted him onto a stake and forked him over the fire. Flames ran up his legs to his chest. Slocum opened his eyes. He was still lying on the ground. He had dreamed the burning stake. How long before the dream would come true?

He closed his eyes and passed out again.

Slocum felt the sensation of being lifted by the arms. Two braves were dragging him across the ground. His vision was blurred, so he could not tell where they were taking him. This might be the end after all.

They dropped him and then rolled him on his side.

Slocum looked up at a dark shape against the sky. It was almost dawn, light enough for him to see the Indian. Tall and broad, the figure had to belong to Red Buck. He was a damned ugly son of a bitch.

A shorter brave stood next to Red Buck. He leaned over to look at Slocum. He said something in Apache. Red Buck replied in the same harsh tongue.

The shorter brave knelt down next to Slocum. "Red Buck says he wanted to see the man who almost escaped him."

Slocum coughed. He couldn't believe the brave was speaking English to him. He thought it was another dream. He closed his eyes. Red Buck kicked him in the stomach.

Slocum almost blacked out. But then the Indian was there, talking to him like any white man. He said that Red Buck wanted to know if more troops would come to Apache territory. He wanted an answer before they killed the tall man.

Slocum's only hope was to confuse Red Buck. Do something he wasn't expecting. What did he have to lose?

He coughed and spat blood onto the ground. "Tell Red Buck he can kiss my ass."

The interpreter frowned. "What?"

"Kiss my ass. He can kiss my ass."

The translation was rendered. Slocum braced for the kick in the ribs, but it never came. Red Buck said something in Apache.

The other brave bent low again. "Red Buck wants to know why you want him to kiss your ass."

"He tied me up," Slocum said. "Chased me. Hurt me. Treated me like a dog. He's gonna kill me, so I'm not gonna tell him anythin'."

The translation was made. Red Buck laughed. He motioned for the translator to cut the rawhide strips that bound the tall man.

When Slocum was loose, he tried to stand up. His head spun. His legs felt weak. He had to sit down again.

Red Buck spoke in his guttural voice. The interpreter asked the same question as before. Slocum just shook his head.

"I won't tell him anythin' till he follows through on the deal," the tall man challenged. "He owes me."

"Why?"

Slocum lifted his eyes toward the big renegade. Red Buck's face was scarred and angry. He also had wounds on his arms and legs. The soldiers must have put up quite a fight before the Apaches massacred them.

Red Buck barked again.

"He wants to know why he owes you and what he owes you," the translator said. "Tell him."

"Those cows," Slocum replied. "I brought 'em to the Apaches. You took 'em. And I know you got the gold from those soldiers. That gold is mine."

"Why should he give it to you?"

"I never did anythin' to Red Buck. I always respected the ways of the red man. Why shouldn't he give me the same in return?"

The words were changed into the Apache language.

Red Buck glared at the audacious trail rider in front of him. Slocum still wondered if the bluff would work. He had to punch it one more time.

"Ask Red Buck if he's a man of honor."

The renegade listened and then nodded.

"I brought the cows and I want my gold," Slocum insisted.

The two Indians spoke back and forth.

"Red Buck says the white man does not have his honor. The white man knows no honor himself."

"Then Red Buck is just like the white man," Slocum challenged. "He's no better'n any paleface."

Red Buck did not appreciate that assertion. But he did not kick the aching drifter. Instead, he receded into the shadows for a few moments, returning with a small strongbox that bore the gold letters of the U.S. Army. Red Buck threw the box in front of Slocum. Then he bellowed another command.

"The gold is yours," the translator said. "Now, are there any more troops coming here?"

Slocum squinted at the brave. "Where'd you learn the white man's tongue?"

"From the fathers at the mission in Pima. I lived there when I was a boy, before I began to follow my great leader."

Slocum cast his green eyes on Red Buck. "Yeah, he looks like a great one, all right. Tell him there's no more troops in Pima. But there'll be plenty up this way if he keeps on with this devilment."

Red Buck laughed when he heard the translation. He said that no soldiers could stop him from raising the Apache nation again. He would ride against the white eyes and defeat them.

Slocum reached for the strongbox. He wasn't going to argue with Red Buck. They watched as he stood up.

"I'm goin'," he said. "A deal is a deal. Tell Red Buck that we're even on the cows."

He could barely lift the strongbox.

Red Buck laughed. He clapped his hands and a circle of braves formed around the tall man from Georgia. Slocum glanced toward Red Buck. He asked if the renegade was going back on their bargain. The translator replied that Slocum would have his gold. He'd just never get a chance to spend it.

The sun beat down on the rock where Slocum had been tied. He hung there by his arms, draped over the angles of a jutting crag at the crest of a rise. The rock faced south, catching most of the sun.

Slocum felt the hot stone on his back. He could lie flat against the crag to keep his arms from dislocating at the shoulder. The Apaches had been careful to strap him so he would have to die of exposure. If he died too soon, the torture would not be as hideous. It had to be slow, Apache-style.

He wondered if they would come back to look at him from time to time. Or would they just leave him? Would he never see another man before he died?

His green eyes rolled up to the sky. Buzzards circled overhead. They'd come to pluck his head clean, arriving before death, probably. As long as he had his voice, he could holler to scare them off.

His mouth was dry. His tongue would swell after he hadn't drunk for a while. He could barely swallow now.

He rolled his head to the right. The strongbox hung next to him. The renegade had kept his word. Slocum had the gold. It was hanging right there.

He laughed. The chortle brought a pain to his chest. He shook on the rock, trying to loosen his rawhide bonds. His whole body ached, so he had to stop shaking.

The sun caused him to pass out. He opened his eyes again in the cool air of dusk. He had not died during the day. The buzzards had not come to pick out his eyes.

The tall man had strange ideas in his head. He wished he could fly like a buzzard, flap his wings and soar right off the hateful ridge. A deep, desperate shriek escaped from his chest. He had to cry out one last time, as if anyone could hear him.

He felt the cool stone on his back. It didn't help the pain. Slocum had never known such pain. He closed his eyes for a long time.

The sound of scuffling woke him. He thought he heard low voices. The Apaches had come back to taunt him.

But then he started to fly. He rose off the rock, soaring upward. He flew through the night air to a place where sleep felt a whole lot better.

Slocum could hear the Apache language in his dreams. They seemed to be all around him. Somebody dabbed a wet cloth on his face. He opened his green eyes to see a lined face staring back at him.

He tried to sit up. He was in the Apache camp. Only this time he was inside a tepee. And the face belonged to an Indian woman.

She pushed him back on the bed.

Slocum didn't have the strength to resist her. They had brought him back to torture him some more. Red Buck hadn't seen enough.

The woman lifted a gourd to his lips. Slocum drank the cool water. It eased some of the burning in his throat.

The woman called over her shoulder.

An older man came in after a while. He looked at Slocum and then went out again. The woman gave him more water.

Slocum drifted off after he had quenched his thirst.

When he woke up again, his head was clearer and the old Apache was sitting at his side, staring at him with gray, glassy eyes.

The old man gestured to the gourd. "Water?"

Slocum nodded. The old man lifted the gourd to Slocum's lips. He drained the cup. He felt better, stronger, but his head spun when he tried to sit up.

"Rest," the old man said.

Slocum rolled his green eyes toward the Indian. "Who are you?"

"Gray Buck."

Slocum did not reply.

"Red Buck is my son," the old man went on. "He wants to fight. But I am too old. My people are not strong, not now."

"You're runnin' with your son," Slocum said. "Isn't that the same as fightin'?"

Gray Buck gestured to the air. "No. You are here, on the reservation. My braves got you away from my son. You are safe."

Slocum let out a nervous chortle. "That so? Then I can leave?"

"When you are stronger. My wife and daughters will heal you. Apache medicine is strong. Drink what they give you. Then I will give you a pony and you will leave us."

Slocum eyed the old man, wondering if this was another one of Red Buck's mean tricks.

The woman came back, carrying a steaming bowl in her hands. She fed Slocum while the old man watched. The thick broth tasted of meat and wild herbs. It sent a warmth through Slocum's body. When he had finished eating, he closed his eyes again, sleeping for a long time, dreaming of things that were no longer so dark and frightening.

After three days of Apache medicine, Slocum was on his feet again. He asked for a pony. Gray Buck immediately brought him a stout-looking pinto. Slocum would have to ride bareback, but it was a small price to pay for getting south, away from Apache country.

Gray Buck gave him food and some fresh clothes. Slocum didn't ask where the old Indian had gotten a white man's shirt and pants. He still had to wonder if it was some kind of trick.

Gray Buck pointed south, telling him to follow the ridges of the Gila Basin. He should be able to avoid Red Buck, the old man said. They had come west to the heart of the reservation. If Slocum stayed steady, he could be all the way to the Mexican border in a week.

The tall man swung onto the back of the pony.

Gray Buck told him to wait. He went into the tepee where Slocum had rested during his recovery. When he came out again, he had two leather pouches strung over his shoulder. The pouches were tied together like saddlebags. Gray Buck had to stoop under the weight of the pouches.

He explained that the strongbox had been broken when they opened it to see what was inside. They had found the gold. Gray Buck figured the double eagles belonged to Slocum, since the strongbox had been hanging next to him on the rock. He also gave the tall man a skin full of water and some food.

Slocum strung the pouches at the base of the pony's neck. "I'm obliged to you, Gray Buck."

"Kill my son if you see him."

Slocum nodded, but he hoped he would never see Red Buck again.

He turned the pony south, making his way out of Apache country.

16

The Indian pony was strong. It carried Slocum south, into the dry, barren flats of the Gila Basin. Slocum had to stop during the hot part of the day. He chased the shaded areas to keep cool. After he drank from the skin of water, he gave the pony a whistle-wetter.

In the shade of some tall rocks, Slocum decided to count the gold pieces that Gray Buck had given him. He took the leather pouches from the pony's back. They must have weighed close to a hundred pounds.

He emptied the pouches into the dirt. The gold sparkled against the dust. His first reaction was to look up, to see if anyone was watching him. But there was only a dull, hot wind on the plain. No Indians, no white men to see him count the gold.

His fingers trembled a little as he stacked the gold pieces into piles of ten. Twenty-five small piles totaled five thousand dollars. Two hundred fifty double eagles. They filled the tall man's eyes. It was his fortune, if he could get it out of Indian country.

Slocum leaned back on the rock, staring at the gold. He had seen what this much gold could do to a man's heart. Now it was his heart that pounded inside his chest. He was the one with the greed sickness.

He thought about Pima, about Rosita. Would she still be there waiting for him? He had almost promised to come back for her. What would Garrity do to the girl when Slocum never returned with the gold?

Better try to think straight, he told himself.

He saw Rosita's expectant face. Damn. Why did he remember her so vividly? Usually a woman faded from his mind as soon as he had left her. She had been good to Slocum. He couldn't turn his back on her.

The tall man from Georgia knew it would be a mistake to go back to Pima. Anytime a man changed his path for a woman, it usually meant disaster somewhere down the line. But he couldn't leave her to Garrity. How would the chubby man treat her when Slocum didn't come back?

Returning for her would be tricky, though. He'd have to get in and out of Pima without Garrity seeing him. Or would he?

Maybe he could hide the gold, claim that he barely escaped from Red Buck and the renegades. Who would doubt him? After all, the cavalry had not been able to bring the Apaches to justice. Who would think that Slocum got away with two sacks full of gold? He could say that he had been lucky to save his own life. Red Buck had the gold.

It had to work. It was the only way he could go back to Pima and free Rosita from Garrity. Slocum wished that he had a gun, even a pistol. How would he protect the gold all the way to Pima?

He took three of the double eagles and put them in his pants pocket. If he happened on a chance to buy something, he wouldn't have to dig into the pouches of gold. He quickly began to refill the leather bags. His fingers continued to tremble as the coins filtered through them.

When he had finished tying up the pouches, he looked at the pony. He wished he had a saddle and a pair of saddlebags. On the pony, the leather pouches stood out like tumbleweeds on a clear street. With a saddle, he'd appear to be just another rider on the plain.

Slocum shook his head. No need to think about things that weren't there. He wasn't even sure that the Indian pony would accept a saddle.

He stood up, peering to the south. It was late afternoon. Lines of heat still quavered on the horizon, but it had cooled enough for him to ride on. The pony felt strong and ready to run.

Slocum started the animal at a steady lope. He bounced on the bare back, trying to hold on as best he could. The leather pouches bounced a little as well. His fortune was contained in two bags that wouldn't hold two shovels' worth of desert sand: not exactly an honest-to-God treasure chest.

As he rode, Slocum kept looking back over his shoulder. Despite his lucky escape, he could not forget that Red Buck and his men were somewhere in the area. Surely they would discover that Slocum was no longer hanging on the death crag. Would they think that the tall man had been taken away by evil spirits or would they come looking for him and the gold?

Sweat poured off his brow, stinging his green eyes. The gold had him rattled. Was this the way that rich men worried? Always wondering if some bastard was going to steal their fortunes?

He tried like hell to shake off the jitters. The gold was his one chance for real freedom. He could live like a king in Mexico. Five thousand would hold him for at least twenty years—if he could hang onto it.

The sun began to sink lower in the sky. Slocum drank from the water skin and then ate some of the fry bread that Gray Buck had given him. Funny, how the Indian hadn't wanted any of the white man's gold. Maybe Gray Buck was smart enough to know how dangerous that much gold could be to a man.

Damn the woman. Why had she been so good to him? Rosita was the only reason he was going back to Pima. If not for her, he would have turned due west and headed for California. There was no trouble with renegade Apaches in

San Diego. From there, he could make it down to Tijuana, live on beans and rice and tequila.

But the thought of Rosita pulled him toward Pima.

He guided the pony to the southeast, riding until he saw the cart ahead of him.

Slocum reined back the pony. There seemed to be one man on the cart, which was pulled by a donkey. The man was heading straight toward him. Slocum considered riding around the man, until he considered that the stranger might have something for sale—a gun or a saddle, maybe.

Slocum spurred the pony, heading straight for the stranger and his cart.

Rosita had been watching Miguel and Garrity all day. The two men had been drinking a lot. Miguel would want her in his bedroll that night. But the girl had other plans.

Miguel called in Spanish, telling her to get them some dinner.

Rosita just smiled. She had built a small campfire. Miguel had shot a couple of prairie hens. He expected them to be roasted.

And Rosita was cooperating, at least on the surface. What Miguel and Garrity had not considered was the girl's knowledge of herbs. She sprinkled the hens with something to make both of them sleep. The herb would work quickly, since they were so drunk. She wished she had something strong enough to kill them, but as it stood, she could only make them pass out.

Miguel bellowed again for his dinner. Rosita took the hens from the spit and carried them to her captors. Miguel smiled, telling her that she was a good woman. Garrity also grinned, like he expected something else from her.

The men began to eat. They did not offer Rosita any of the meat. She had some cold bread that served as her supper. She sat by the fire, watching, as the two men filled their bellies.

At first, she was afraid that Miguel might detect the flavor of the sleeping herb, but he was too drunk. How long would it take them to sleep? Darkness would be on them soon. If she could escape under the cover of night, she might be able to go north, to find Slocum.

"Rosita!"

She flinched when she saw Miguel rising to his feet. He motioned for her to follow him. He wanted her to go with him behind the ridge, so Garrity could not watch when Miguel mounted her. She had to obey him or risk a beating from the drunk Mexican.

Miguel staggered as he went before her. When they were behind the ridge, he told her to lie down, to lift her dress. She had to do his bidding.

Why couldn't he pass out before he topped her? Maybe she hadn't used enough of the sleeping herb. She might have gathered the wrong plant on the trail. Sometimes herbs looked alike.

Miguel began to fiddle with the buttons of his fly. He reeled, gazing down at the dark patch between Rosita's thighs. He took out his limp cock. He told Rosita to touch it.

As she was reaching for him, Miguel stumbled and fell. His weight pressed her against the ground. She expected him to start humping, but Miguel did not move.

Rosita rolled him off her. He was finally asleep. She pulled her dress down and got to her feet, praying that Garrity was no longer conscious.

Sure enough, as she came over the ridge, she saw the chubby man sprawled on the ground. The liquor and the herb had done him in. She grabbed the reins of Miguel's horse, climbing into the saddle. Turning the animal north, she started away from their camp.

For a while, she considered going into Pima, to tell the soldiers where to find Miguel and Garrity.

But something told her to bypass the small town. She wanted to get north, to find Slocum. She just hoped it wasn't too late to help the man she loved.

The man with the cart stopped when he saw Slocum approaching in the soft light of dusk. Slocum kept his hands high, so the man could see that he wasn't going to pull a gun on him. The man nodded politely to Slocum as he rode up on the pony.

Slocum nodded back. "Howdy, mister."

The man squinted up at him. "Ridin' bareback, huh? Reckon that's tough on a man."

The tall man slid off the pony's back. He stretched, working the kinks out of his back. The man in the cart watched him. He probably didn't trust the man on the Indian pony. Slocum wouldn't have trusted himself, either, on this lonely Arizona plain.

"You're a long way from home," the man said.

Slocum exhaled. "More'n you know, stranger."

"Name's Hubbins. You got a name?"

"John."

"John what?"

Slocum shrugged. "Just John."

Hubbins nodded. He appeared to be a grizzled, worn-out prospector. Gold pans and a pickax hung from the sides of the cart. Hubbins probably hadn't shaved in a year. Several teeth were missing from his mouth.

"Where you headin'?" he asked.

Slocum squinted at the man. "Where you comin' from?"

"Nogales," Hubbins replied. "Headin' up this way to see if I can't stake a claim on some silver."

Slocum looked away, figuring he had the man where he wanted him. Old prospectors were always short on money. Why would Hubbins be different?

"Look here, old-timer, there's some things I need. I'm willin' to pay. You lookin' for a grubstake?"

Hubbins nodded, rubbing his chin. "Always lookin' for a grubstake, sir. But I ain't got nothin' to sell you."

"No guns?" Slocum asked.

The prospector glanced at the pony and then at Slocum. He could see that the tall man wasn't packing iron. Slocum figured the old boy wouldn't draw on him. Slocum could take him easily even if Hubbins tried to pull a pistol.

"I need a gun," the tall man repeated. "Don't care what kind. Pistol, rifle, scattergun. I'm willin' to pay."

Hubbins laughed. "Pardner, you look as busted as me. If you want to buy a gun, you need money."

Slocum silenced him by pulling a double eagle out of his pocket. The gold glinted in the last rays of daylight. Hubbins gaped wide-eyed at the coin. Slocum figured it had been a long time since the man had seen a twenty-dollar gold piece.

Hubbins stammered a little. "I—er, I mean—I ain't got

a gun that's worth twenty dollars, mister."

"If you got any gun that'll shoot, it's worth twenty dollars to me. If not, I'll be ridin' on."

Hubbins didn't want him to leave. "Now hold on, stranger. I do have a pistol, but it's pretty rusty."

"Does it shoot?"

Hubbins started to reach into the cart. "Here, let me—"

Slocum grabbed his hand. "I'll get it."

"But—"

Slocum peered into the man's frightened eyes. "Wouldn't want you to try to plug me for this gold, Hubbins."

"Okay, it's right under that piece of cloth."

Slocum rummaged around until he found the rusty Colt. It was a percussion cap model. Hubbins hadn't even loaded it.

"You got powder and caps?" the tall man asked.

Hubbins nodded again. "Should be a box where you found the gun."

The old prospector was right. Slocum lifted the box from the cart. He began to load the rusty weapon.

"Never keep it ready myself," Hubbins said. "Hell, I can't shoot the broadside of a barn."

"Aren't you afraid of thieves and murderers?" Slocum asked.

Hubbins laughed nervously. "Well, you could say that I'm hopin' you ain't one."

Slocum brandished the Colt, holding it at arm's length. He thumbed back the hammer and let off one shot. The pistol sent a slug careening over the dusty plain. Dirt kicked up where the bullet had hit.

He looked back at the prospector who had begun to sweat. "Twenty dollars," he said. "Okay by you?"

The man nodded. "That's ten times what I paid for it. Hell, I never even shot it once. Never even loaded it. But I figured a man needs a gun out here. So I bought it down in Mexico."

Slocum gestured toward the wagon. "You wouldn't have a saddle in there, would you?"

Hubbins laughed. "Never owned a ridin' horse since I was a younger man. Don't make enough prospectin' to feed this burro."

The donkey made Slocum think of Rosita. She had followed the trail drive on her little burro. He had to go back to Pima to get her. Once he rescued her from Garrity, he could take her back to Dos Cabezas to her people.

"How 'bout some whiskey?" Slocum asked.

"Ain't got none to sell," Hubbins replied. "Less'n you count Mexican rotgut. I'll be happy to give you a swig, but I couldn't rightly sell it to you. Ain't worth a dime."

Slocum said the Mexican rotgut would be fine with him. He watched as Hubbins reached into the cart. He almost expected the old boy to come up with a rifle or a shotgun. But the prospector produced a crock jug.

"I think they make this stuff out of cactus juice and horse piss," Hubbins remarked. "Only in this batch, they left out the cactus juice." He laughed at his own joke.

Slocum did not crack a smile. He drank some of the foul-tasting brew. It burned and made his head spin.

Hubbins kept smiling. "You didn't say where you's headin'."

"No, I didn't."

The old prospector shrugged. "Man's got a right to go his own way. I ain't one to—"

Slocum started to move toward the Indian pony.

"Hey," Hubbins called, "you never—"

Slocum turned to throw him the gold piece. Hubbins missed the coin which fell into the dust. The old man picked it up and examined it carefully.

"Real, all right," he said. "Twenty dollars for that old gun. I reckon this is my lucky day."

Slocum didn't care two hoots about the old man's luck. He slid onto the pony's bare back. Turning the animal to the southwest again, he drove hard toward the darkening horizon. He had to get to Pima, to find the girl. The tall man wanted to finish his business with Rosita. Then he'd have time to figure out what he was going to do with his newfound fortune.

17

The Indian pony seemed to be used to walking at night. It carried Slocum through the rolling hills of the basin, never stumbling, tirelessly plodding to the south. The tall man simply had to hang on and let the animal do all the work. He'd probably make Pima by morning, if the pony held up.

Slocum knew he'd have to stop to rest himself. His back ached and his tailbone was numb. He had a new respect for the Apaches. Any man who could ride without a saddle had to be tough.

But the pony wouldn't let him rein up. Instead, the pinto broke into a steady run, driving over a sudden plateau of flat ground. Slocum had to grab its mane to keep from falling off.

After covering a half mile, the pinto slowed and then stopped in the darkness. Slocum heard the bubbling water of the stream. It had to be the the upper reaches of the Gila River. He was closer to Pima than he had figured. It wouldn't hurt to rest a while.

Slocum slid off the pinto's back. His legs were weak and wobbly. He steadied himself against the mount, wishing he had some more of Gray Buck's Indian medicine.

Falling on hands and knees, Slocum drank from the cool stream. He dunked his head in the water to revive himself. His head spun a little.

He ate what was left of the food that the Apache had given him. His stomach settled some, but his head still ached.

He gazed south along the riverbank. A thin stand of brush was clumped at the bend, where the stream began a sinuous curving. Slocum walked the pony to the brush, hobbling it so he could get some sleep. He would just close his eyes for a while. Maybe the pain would go away.

The dry ground would have to serve as a bedroll, but Slocum didn't care. He stretched out in the center of the brush pile. Something slithered away from the clump, but the tall man didn't even notice it.

Slocum wasn't sure he had heard the snapping twig. He sat up from a deep sleep, drawing the old pistol from his pants. The pony had probably been foraging. Had he heard it eating?

Someone moved in the brush. It had to be a man. There were no bears in this part of Arizona, so it had to be the only other thing that moved upright.

The old prospector, Slocum thought. He had come back to kill him. He knew that Slocum had plenty of gold.

The pony snorted.

Slocum thumbed back the hammer of the pistol.

A dark shape appeared over the back of the pony. Then the figure moved around in front of the animal. He hadn't even seen Slocum sleeping a few feet away.

The tall man scrambled to his feet.

The intruder heard him and turned to face the Colt.

Slocum looked into the wide eyes of an Apache brave. The warrior started to cry out, but the report of the rusty pistol echoed in the low reaches of the river basin. Buckling forward, the Indian fell to the ground, clutching his chest.

Slocum watched him die. He shook a lot before he drew his last breath.

The tall man lifted his green eyes to the darkness, anticipating the rush of Apaches who would come to help their fallen cohort. He had five shots left. He could get a few of them before they did him in.

But the Apaches never came. There was only silence, except for the rushing of the Gila River. Slocum moved cautiously toward the pony. Another warrior could be lurking anywhere in the shadows.

Why had the dead Apache been so careless?

The pony, Slocum told himself. He had figured Slocum to be one of his own. No white man rode a bareback pinto. The Indian had been damned surprised to see the pistol staring back at him.

Slocum reached to unhobble the pinto. His head bobbed up. Another horse snorted somewhere in the night. It had to be the dead Indian's mount. Or else his brothers had come to help him.

The horse snorted again. Slocum lifted the pistol and moved slowly through the brush. Best just to fight it out, he thought. The Apaches would get him sooner or later. He wanted to go out shooting.

The brush rustled to his left. Slocum turned with the pistol, drawing down on a tall horse. When he got closer to the mount, he saw that it had a saddle on it. It was the roan that Bill had been riding. That meant the dead Apache was from the same group of Indians who had attacked the trail drive, the same ones who had staked out Slocum and left him for the buzzards.

He turned in a circle, scouting the murky plain. Where the hell were the others? Why would a lone Apache be riding the Gila River without help?

Slocum decided not to worry about it. He untied the roan and led it back into the brush. The horse even had saddlebags, which Slocum emptied in a hurry. He transferred the gold into the bags and then threw them over the back of the roan.

It felt good to climb into a saddle. He turned away from the dead Indian, leaving the pony to run free. As he galloped south, along the bank of the river, he half expected the whole

Apache nation to come after him. But there were no hostiles on his trail. Just a breeze that blew him toward Pima.

He decided to ride straight through. He'd reach the town before sunlight, which meant that he could rest a while before he went searching for the girl. What if she had already left for another town? Slocum wouldn't mind that a bit, he decided. He could move on with his fortune.

The roan held as steady as the pony. He tried not to think about the dead boys. Slocum hadn't been wrong to run like he did. He had just been a little quicker and luckier than Bill and Cal. No more, no less.

He reached back to touch the saddlebags full of gold. So much money put worries into a man's head. Having it brought on thoughts of losing it. A man didn't have to go far in Arizona to find somebody to rob him.

Slocum considered just giving it all to Garrity, taking his five hundred, and running to Mexico. But the gold had been delivered to the tall man and he intended to have the whole pile. He'd take something for himself, for a change.

The roan finally ascended a rise overlooking Pima.

Slocum's eyes strained to pick out the vague shapes of the community. He could see the abandoned mission and the general store. The stable was dark, but a light burned in the army post.

The tall man dismounted on the crest of the ridge. He kept peering toward the army post. Had the soldiers come to Pima?

He was too far away to see if there were horses in the corrals. The pens were just black circles in the distance. He'd have to wait until the sun came up.

Sitting on the ground, he closed his eyes, dozing until the dawn broke to the east. Slocum got up, gazing at Pima in the light of day. The tall man wasn't sure he liked what he saw. The corral closest to the army building was full of strong mounts. And a cavalry flag had been raised over the camp.

Where were the soldiers' tents? They had to raise canvas if they were going to bivouac—unless they were staying in the mission. He squinted, trying to pick out the sentries. There they were, one man each in front of the mission and the outpost. The soldiers had come north from Fort Bowie to help out the squad that had been looking for Red Buck.

The tall man felt the sweat break over his brow. He didn't want to mess with the army. The soldiers probably knew that somebody had taken the cows to the Indians. They'd go up to look for their men sooner or later. Slocum sure as hell didn't want to be around when they started combing the countryside.

He turned away, leading the horse down the incline. The tall man could not even remember why he had come to Pima. He wanted to go around it, make sure nobody saw him.

Having been a soldier himself, Slocum tried to think like a bluecoat. They'd have patrols out, riding in all directions. Cavalry always put out riders to scout the area, even if they were just looking for water or securing their range of operation. Maybe it would be better to wait until dark before he circled around Pima.

If he waited, he'd have to find a place to hide. There were plenty of rocks along the river. He could ride back and find shade, get some sleep, then ride on at dark, when it was safer.

He could feel his heart inside his chest. He touched the heavy bags on the back of the roan. It was almost too damned much trouble to protect his fortune. Almost.

Slocum leaned back against the damp rock. There was an overhang above him to provide shade. The river ran in front of him and the roan. He had used some smaller rocks to tie the animal. It wasn't a bad place to rest. The bank was high and steep. A man would have to ride right up on him to see him in this hiding place.

His eyes closed. He slept with the saddlebags at his side. When he finally woke, he saw a shape standing against the light. He lifted the pistol, thinking that the Apache had come back to haunt him.

"No, Slocum, it's me!"

He focused on the girl. "Rosita?"

She dropped next to him, putting her head on his chest. In a sobbing voice, she told him how much she had missed him.

Slocum couldn't believe she had been able to find him.

"What happened in Pima?" he asked her.

She told him about Miguel and Garrity, about how they had run when the soldiers arrived. They hadn't wanted to face the army. Garrity felt he had bungled the cattle deal, anyway.

He looked into her dark eyes. "Why'd Miguel show up?"

"He wan' more money."

Slocum shook his head, exhaling. "Damn. Miguel and Garrity. If it wasn't bad enough with those damned blue-coats showin' up."

Rosita drew back a little. "You ha' the gold."

His brow fretted. "Rosita—"

"I can see in your face. You ha' the gold."

Her dark eyes fell on the saddlebags.

Slocum nodded reluctantly. "Yeah, I got it. Had to fight the devil to do it, but here it is."

She frowned. "Wa' stole from my people!"

"Yeah, I reckon. But it's mine, now. If I can get it south."

Rosita turned away, rising to her feet. She was crying. Slocum felt badly, but he didn't say a word. Rosita had to be a big girl, to take her medicine like anybody else who went riding wild asses all over the Arizona Territory. The game didn't have rules for soft women. Everybody who played took it on the chin sooner or later.

The girl began to unbutton her dress. He watched as she dropped the garment and then waded into the river. She washed in the current, her hair billowing around her in the current. When she had rinsed, she walked out onto the bank again, staring down at Slocum.

He could see the bruises on her smooth skin. "Did Miguel hurt you?"

"He try."

She motioned to the lanky man from Dixie. "You. Een the river an' I weel lie wi' you."

Slocum shook his head. "It's not gonna work, Rosita. You won't get me to give up this gold like that."

Her thick lips parted. "I don' care. I wan' you."

He wanted her as well.

The tall man removed his clothes and waded into the river. Rosita slid next to him in the cool current. Their bodies entwined. He could feel her against his hardness.

Slocum picked her up, carrying her to the sandy bank. He put her on her back, falling between her legs. Rosita raised her butt, accepting him. They humped on the sand until both had found their pleasure.

Slocum kissed her generous mouth. She had him. Rosita was too sweet to leave behind. He could think of worse traveling companions.

She squirmed out from under him. Her dress needed washing. She scrubbed it in the river as he watched. When she was finished with her own laundry, she insisted on washing Slocum's clothes. He didn't protest. He was trying to figure a way to tell her that she could ride south with him.

"Look here, Rosita—"

She gazed back at him from the river.

He sighed. "Well, I just figger that part of that gold is yours. You sweated as much as me on this thing."

She looked away. "I don' wan' your gold."

"Take your share. How 'bout five hundred dollars? You can do what you want with the money. Give it to your people."

"No."

He couldn't convince her to ride south with him. When he asked her what she was going to do, Rosita would not reply. She simply spread the wet clothes on some rocks so they could dry in the heat. She sat there, staring at nothing, her eyes wide and vacant.

When the clothes were dry, they dressed again. Slocum tried to kiss her, but she would not let him. There was no getting through to her.

The tall man turned away from Rosita. He didn't care what she wanted. The gold was his, and nobody was going to take his fortune away from him.

He raised his eyes to the sky. It was late afternoon, maybe two hours until dark. There would probably be a moon. He'd have to be careful, even after the sun went down.

Slocum figured to offer the girl one more chance to ride with him. He started to turn toward her. A shadow came between him and the sun. Rosita was there, swinging a rock at him.

He tried to dodge the blow but she had been too quick.

The rock caught him as it brushed his temple. He fell to the ground, losing consciousness.

Slocum sat up, gazing at the blue-coated lieutenant. The soldier was blurry. He rode a tall, black stallion. Slocum could see the other shapes behind the lieutenant. They were also on horseback.

"May I ask your name, sir?" the soldier said.

Slocum glanced to his right, looking for the girl and his mount. Both were gone. Rosita had run off after she whacked him. Slocum touched the dried blood on the side of his head.

The young lieutenant frowned at him. "You seem to be injured, sir. Would you require assistance?"

Slocum shook his head. "No. Just leave me be."

"I'm afraid I can't do that, sir. We're patrolling for hostiles in this area, so it has been closed off to all civilians. You, sir, are a civilian, so I'm afraid I'll have to ask you to come with us to Pima. There's a garrison of troops there. You'll be quite safe."

Slocum glared back at the man. "I don't have a horse."

"Were you waylaid by Apaches?"

"I can't remember."

"Perhaps you will. Now, if you'll come with us. You can ride double with one of my men."

What could he do? If things weren't bad enough already, he had to be captured by the cavalry. Rosita had taken his gold. At least the soldiers weren't the Apaches. Still, Slocum found little consolation in knowing that the blue-coated riders were on his side.

18

Slocum rode behind a corporal on a tall bay. They ate dust until they reached Pima. The six riders reined up outside the general store. The storekeeper sat on the porch in a wooden chair.

"Is the colonel here?" the young lieutenant asked.

The storekeeper glanced up at the tall man who rode double. He stared straight at Slocum.

The tall man lowered his head, hiding behind the corporal.

The lieutenant seemed to grow impatient. "I asked if the colonel is here, sir."

"No, he ain't," the proprietor replied. "Say, that you, Mr. Slocum?"

Slocum turned his green eyes away. "Ain't my name."

"Shucks, if you don't look just like the boy that took them cows north to the reservation."

The lieutenant's suspicious leer fell on the tall man. "He can't remember who he is. As you see, he's sustained a wound on the head. It's called amnesia. I studied about it when I was at West Point."

"That's the man," the storekeeper offered. "Rode out with two boys and never come back."

Slocum eyed the grinning fool. He hadn't mentioned Garrity. The chubby man had probably paid him not to say a word, to sell Slocum down the river.

The lieutenant looked at the corporal. "Take this man to the colonel's office right away. Colonel Barton will want to interrogate him."

Slocum considered a move right then, but there were too many of them surrounding him. The corporal didn't have a sidearm for him to steal. He could knock him off the saddle, but somebody else would have gotten him with a slug.

The corporal turned the bay toward the outpost. Several men, including the lieutenant, fell in beside them. The others made for the mission to secure their mounts.

Slocum climbed down in front of the outpost. Two soldiers grabbed him, ushering him into the main office of the cabin. A bearded man in a blue officer's coat sat behind a large desk. Slocum stood in front of the man.

"Explain this, Lieutenant," the bearded officer said in a booming voice.

The subordinate officer snapped to attention. "Sir, our patrol found this man wounded beside the Gila River. We believe that he was the man who took the herd of cattle north, toward the reservation. However, he seems to have sustained a head injury that precludes him from remembering anything, including his name and whereabouts."

Colonel Cornelius Barton leaned back and folded his hands over his chest. "Is that so?"

His steely eyes burned straight through the tall man. Slocum knew he would lose if he matched wits with the old man, but there was a way to string it out, maybe get what he needed. He'd have to rely on the truth, though, or at least part of the truth.

"Has his head wound been attended?"

The lieutenant shook his head. "He declined treatment, sir."

Barton leaned forward, putting his hands on the desk. "Well, son, what do you have to say for yourself?"

Slocum touched his head, where the girl had hit him. "Can I have a shot of whiskey, Colonel Barton?"

The request did not seem to bother the colonel. He looked at the lieutenant, who bristled like a bantam rooster.

They were pretty sharp, Slocum thought, even if they were Yankees.

"That will be all, Lieutenant."

The rooster's beak dropped a little. "Sir, I—"

A wave from the colonel. "You did a fine job, Lieutenant. But I want to talk to this man alone."

"Yes, sir." Most of the lieutenant's luster had been restored with the compliment. He wheeled and marched out of the room.

As soon as he was gone, the colonel produced a bottle of whiskey and two tin cups. He poured them both half full and then handed one to Slocum.

The tall man emptied the cup quickly. It spread a warmth over him. His head loosened some. If he was going to spill it out, he had to stay close to what really happened.

"How did you sustain that wound, son?"

Slocum looked straight at him. "That's not what you want to know, Colonel."

"I see."

"You got other questions," Slocum continued. "My head's clear enough to give 'em to you."

Barton nodded. "All right. More whiskey?"

Slocum took another shot. Yes, the truth would set him free. He wouldn't have to tell it all, but he'd give up enough to make the old boy happy.

"You ask me anythin', Colonel. But I haven't done anythin' wrong. What happened wasn't my fault."

"Fair enough."

The tall man from Georgia took a deep breath. "I also want your guarantee that you'll give me a horse and let me get the hell out of Indian country as soon as possible."

Colonel Barton shook his head. "No guarantees, no promises. You tell me what you know, and we'll see."

Slocum didn't have much choice. "Okay, Colonel. What do you want to know?"

Barton eyed the solemn rebel. "Are you, or are you not the man who drove that herd of cows north to the reservation?"

Slocum nodded. "I am."

"What's your name?"

His green eyes narrowed. "Wouldn't you like to know about the troops you got up there? The ones that were chasin' Red Buck?"

"What happened to them?"

He lowered his head. "They aren't chasin' him anymore."

"They caught him?"

"No. Red Buck caught them."

He told the officer about the bodies he had found in the hills. He left out the part about hiding in the stack of bodies. Some truths just didn't have to be said. Not if it made Slocum look bad.

"My God," Barton replied. "You saw them all dead?"

"Every one. Red Buck got the herd, too. He killed those two boys that were with me. They weren't fast enough."

Barton stood and began to pace back and forth. "How many warriors does Red Buck have with him?"

Slocum shrugged. "Fifty."

"Three times the original report. Do they all have rifles?"

"Maybe half of 'em."

Barton eyed Slocum. "Sir, you have an officer's eye for detail. Have you ever served in the army?"

The lanky Georgian stiffened proudly. "I rode for the army of the Confederacy, sir."

Barton didn't have much to say to that.

He started pacing again. "Drat! Fifty braves. Were you in the Apache camp?"

"Yes."

"How'd you escape?"

Slocum told him about Gray Buck's rescue.

Colonel Barton raised a hand. "Aha! I knew it. Most of the Apaches don't want to fight. If we can just cut the head off the snake, get Red Buck before he makes any more trouble—"

Slocum leaned back a little. "He's gonna make more trouble, sir. You can be sure of that."

Barton stopped to glare at him again. "Did you work for the man named Garrity?"

"I did. Last I seen of him, he was sittin' on the porch of the general store. We had some trouble with a man name of Rattman. Garrity got wounded, elseways he'd have been up there with the herd. Wasn't he still here when you came with your troops?"

Barton shook his head. "Haven't seen him."

Slocum shrugged. "That's all I know, Colonel. 'Cept that I'm lucky to be alive."

"You can tell me more. Where did you last see Red Buck and his men?"

"Up above Apache Wells. Only—"

Barton frowned. "Go on."

Slocum told him about the Apache brave he had killed in the dark. There might be a war party close by. The warrior could have been a scout.

"You seem to have a knack for getting in and out of trouble," the colonel said. "Unless you're lying."

"Why would I lie, Colonel?"

"Gold," the old man replied. "Five thousand dollars in double eagles. The money targeted for the herd of cows that was going to Gray Buck."

Slocum tried to look calm and unconcerned. "I never ran into any gold, sir. Red Buck might have it. He killed your men."

"Damn that renegade!"

Barton had bought it. Slocum wondered what good it would do. Rosita had the double eagles—except for the two left in Slocum's pocket. He had almost forgotten about the coins he had taken from the leather pouches. Now Rosita roamed the plain, probably heading south with his saddlebags, stealing the gold that had almost gotten him killed.

Barton glanced out the window. "I'll have to go after Red Buck. It's almost dusk now. My men and I will pull out first thing in the morning."

Slocum figured if the colonel waited long enough, Red Buck would come to him. But he didn't say anything. He wasn't in the army now. He just wanted to get the hell out of Pima.

"I can field sixty men," Barton went on. "Do you think that will be enough to face the renegades?"

Slocum grimaced. "Why the hell you askin' me?"

"Man to man. Tell me."

Slocum thought about it, then replied, "They better be tough men."

Barton nodded. "Very well. You've been straight with me, sir. Take your pick of a mount from our remuda. You may leave at once. I can't blame you for wanting to be shed of Apache country."

The generosity caught the green-eyed rebel off guard. He had expected the colonel to detain him. Now maybe he'd have a chance to catch Rosita. He wanted his fortune back.

He figured he should offer the colonel one more piece of advice. "Sir?"

"Yes?"

Slocum sighed. "Well, just don't go back in those hills lookin' for Red Buck. Wait'll he comes out himself. You hear me?"

"I assure you that I can take care of the situation," Barton replied. "Now, if you'll excuse me, I have to see to my men."

Slocum didn't have to be told twice. He strode out of the office, heading back to the general store. The young lieutenant fell in beside him.

"What did the colonel say?"

Slocum looked straight ahead. "Said I'm to have my pick of the horses from the remuda."

"Is that it?"

"Y'all are leavin' tomorrow mornin' for Indian territory. Gonna have a look for Red Buck."

The lieutenant stopped dead in his tracks. "Indian country?"

Slocum just kept walking. He felt sort of good about getting a rise from the shavetail bluecoat. He sure as hell didn't envy the young officer. Slocum knew just how tough the renegades could be.

He walked on to the general store. The storekeeper flinched when Slocum came in. He was surprised that the army had released the tall man so quickly. Fear spread across the man's weak face.

"Slocum, I—"

The lanky rebel strode across the store, putting his hand on a saddle that rested against the wall.

"Slocum, I swear, I thought they knew who you were. Garrity told me not to say anything about him."

"What about the Mexican?" Slocum said.

"He left with Garrity."

Slocum grabbed the saddle. "I'm takin' this."

"Well, I—"

Slocum glared at him. "Garrity paid you off not to say a word. This is my payoff for not tellin' him how you sold me out."

"But I—"

He walked out of the store with the saddle in front of him.

Darkness had fallen over Pima, but Slocum planned to leave as soon as he could saddle a mount.

The soldiers were mustering for roll call and to receive their orders. They had gathered in front of the mission. If they were good cavalrymen and if they waited for the renegade to come down out of the hills, they probably would be able to stop Red Buck.

When he reached the remuda, the lieutenant was already there, cutting a horse out of the herd. He led a short, black gelding to the edge of the corral. It didn't look like a bad mount.

"He's thrown a shoe," the lieutenant said. "And the other one on the front is broken."

Slocum's brow fretted at the young officer. "Damn. How come you got to give me that one?"

"Because I'll need the others for my men. Take the horse to the stable and have the shoes fixed. Tell the liveryman to put it on our account."

Slocum couldn't argue. It would mean a couple of wasted hours before he could start after Rosita. He took the rope tether and led the black horse toward the livery.

He had to wake the stableman, whose eyes grew wide. "Slocum! You're here! I'm glad to see you."

Slocum started to tell the man about the bad shoes on the black, but the liveryman didn't seem to be listening. He peered nervously at the tall man, his worried eyes catching the orange glow of an oil lamp.

"Slocum—"

"Fix those shoes tonight."

"I will, but you got to come with me. To the back. Come on, I got to show you somethin'."

Slocum realized that he no longer had the pistol in his belt. Rosita must have taken it. The bitch had left him without a firearm.

"Slocum—"

"I'm stayin' right here, honcho. If you got somethin' to show me, you go get it."

"Aw, hell." He looked back into the shadows. "Come on out. He's here."

A door hinge creaked. Slocum saw the dark figure moving in the eerie light. Rosita walked into the glow of the lamp.

"You!"

Her eyes were blank. She shook her head. Slocum grabbed her arms.

"Rosita, where's my gold? What'd you—"

"No, Slocum, don' say eet!"

But it was too late.

Two more shadows moved from the same back room.

The liveryman smiled. "Your friends came back, Mr. Slocum. They was waitin' for you to ride through."

Slocum saw both of them clearly. He recognized Garrity's chubby face. And he knew the dark, swarthy man with the rifle had to be Rosita's old boyfriend, the Mexican known as Miguel.

19

Slocum watched as Garrity tipped back his high hat. His arm was still in a sling. He held a derringer in his good hand. Slocum had seen the weapon before.

Miguel toted a Winchester. He had an angry look on his dark face. He spat at Slocum.

"You are the peeg who stole my Rosita!"

The girl stood, head down, in front of him.

Miguel pushed her down at Slocum's feet. "Go to your greengo! There he ees. You love heem!"

Slocum had a mean glint in his green eyes. "Last time I saw you, Miguel, you were pushin' around this same woman. You ever try to bull anybody your own size?"

The Mexican growled and lifted the Winchester.

"Miguel!" Garrity moved over, pushing down the barrel of the gun.

"I weel kill heem!"

"No, you won't," Garrity said. "Slocum's a reasonable man. Tell you what, John, you lead me to the gold, I'll stick by our original deal. You'll see five hundred dollars. I won't even count that two-fifty I gave you before."

Slocum shook his head. "I don't have the gold, Garrity. I barely got away from Red Buck with my life. The other two boys weren't so lucky."

Garrity grimaced. "Red Buck!"

"The renegade," Slocum went on. "He jumped us, took everything. He killed those troops up there. He might be headin' this way."

Miguel jumped forward, swinging the butt of the rifle into Slocum's gut. The tall man went down to his knees. He felt like he was going to puke out his innards. Rosita got up, putting her hands on his shoulders.

"Liar!" Miguel cried. "You have the gold! You say so to the girl when you come een!"

Slocum fought to catch his breath.

Garrity pulled Miguel away from the tall man. "Don't kill him, you dumb bean-eater. If he's dead, we'll never find the gold."

Miguel grumbled, turning away with the rifle.

Garrity stepped in front of Slocum. "Look here, reb, there's no need for this. I'm gonna pay you."

"I didn't get any gold," Slocum insisted.

Garrity looked at the girl. "You asked her about it first thing when you saw her. Isn't that right, honey?"

Slocum coughed and then raised his green eyes. "She picked my pockets out there on the plain. I had a few double eagles left from the money you gave me. Red Buck didn't get it all."

Garrity's eyes narrowed. "You saw Red Buck?"

"He strung me out to dry," Slocum said. "His daddy was good enough to save me. Turned me loose. Red Buck's got all your gold."

The chubby man frowned. "Slocum, I don't believe you. You'd never get away from Red Buck."

"Ask the colonel," the tall man challenged. "He's saddlin' his cavalry tomorrow, headin' out to face the renegade."

Garrity looked at Miguel. "It's lookin' bad."

The Mexican came forward with the rifle again. "I say we shoot heem!"

Slocum lowered his eyes. He still had one chance. Rosita had hidden the gold somewhere and she had not told the others about it. They thought Slocum knew where to find the saddlebags full of double eagles. If he could get out of this with Rosita, she might lead him to the gold.

"Keel heem!" the Mexican cried again.

Garrity didn't seem as disagreeable now. "We might have to torture him. He'll be almost dead by the time he tells us."

Miguel glared at the girl. "She knows. He ask her where ees the gold. She can tell us."

Garrity turned to Rosita. "You got somethin' to say, girl?"

She had a fearful gleam in her eyes. "No, I don' know. He tol' the truth. I pick hees pocket."

Miguel started to grab her. Garrity held him back. He told the Mexican that he had something else in mind.

"Don't get too close to that reb," Garrity went on. "He's quicker'n he looks. Tough, too. But I think I got a way to make him talk."

Slocum lifted his face again. "There isn't any gold, Garrity. Give it up. When those soldiers catch Red Buck, they'll have it all. You can get it from them. Hell, I delivered those cows."

"I reckon you did," the chubby man replied. "But just in case you aren't tellin' the truth, I'm gonna have to test you. You hear me?"

Slocum didn't move.

Garrity sighed. "I kinda liked you, reb, but I like gold a whole lot better. You can save a lot of time and pain if you'll just take me to where you hid my money."

"There ees no money!" Rosita cried.

Garrity shook his head. "If that's the way you want it— Miguel, get her. Tie her to that beam."

Slocum stood, moving between the girl and Miguel. "Don't hurt her, Garrity. If you're gonna torture somebody, try me."

"You'd take too long, Slocum. But I'm guessin' that a Johnny Reb like you can't stand to hear a girl cry."

The liveryman, who had been silent, stepped into the

circle of light. "Gentlemen, if you're gonna—"

Miguel swung the rifle butt into his forehead. When the man went down, the Mexican didn't stop. He hit him at least five more times.

Slocum started to take a step.

Garrity brandished the derringer. "Don't make me kill you, reb."

The tall man looked him in the eye. "Soldiers may come for their horses to be shod."

"Thanks for tellin' me," Garrity replied. "Miguel. Lock the door, put out a closed sign, if there is one."

The Mexican seemed to take orders pretty well. When the door was locked, he turned down the oil lamp until it was a small speck of yellow. There would be enough light for what they intended to do.

Slocum was afraid they were going to hurt the girl. He watched helplessly as Miguel grabbed her and tied her wrists to the vertical beam. When Miguel ripped away the back part of her dress, Slocum knew he was going to whip her.

Miguel unrolled the bullwhip that he kept in a leather bag. A rustler needed a long whip to get cattle moving in the dark. Slocum figured the Mexican knew how to use the lash.

The tip of the bullwhip cracked in the air.

Slocum looked at the derringer and then at the girl. "Rosita—"

"Don' tell theem, Slocum!"

Garrity backed away, picking up the rifle. "Take it easy on her, Miguel. We wanna string it out. Make him tell us before we kill her."

Miguel rolled the lash in his hand, making circles with the leather. "The first ees always the most painful."

"Puerco!" Rosita cried.

Miguel popped the lash next to her ear. A clump of hair fell away. Slocum saw the blood trickling from her earlobe.

"Rosita!"

He took a step.

Garrity raised the derringer. "One more and you'll be pickin' lead out of your gullet."

Slocum glared at the chubby man. "Don't do this."

"Tell me where to find the gold." Garrity's face turned

hateful. "Tell me, or he takes her eyes after he cuts the blood outta her back."

"No!" Rosita cried.

Miguel furled the lash again. "Puta!"

The whip cracked. A single line of blood trickled down Rosita's back. Slocum stepped between her and Miguel.

"All right," he said. "I'll tell you. I'll lead you straight to the gold. Just don't hurt her anymore."

Garrity smiled. "I knew you'd be reasonable."

"Take us now!" Miguel insisted.

Slocum scowled at the Mexican. "Are you loco? There's fifty cavalry riders out there. And they're all gonna be jumpy tonight. They're leavin' for the Apache reservation tomorrow, first thing in the mornin'. I can take you then. You can wait that long."

"He's stalling!" the Mexican cried.

Garrity rubbed his chubby face. "Well, if he is, then we're sure as hell gonna kill him. Tomorrow mornin', Slocum. You better be able to deliver. Otherwise, you're dead."

"Oww!"

Slocum took the wet cloth away from the lash mark on Rosita's back. They had put them both in the back room, locking it from the outside. The stableman was also lying on the floor of the room. He had not yet regained consciousness, although he was still breathing.

Slocum dipped the cloth in the bucket of water next to his feet. They had climbed onto the stableman's cot. Rosita's body trembled as he dabbed the wound again. Slocum had to give her some credit. She was damned brave to stand up to Garrity and Miguel like she had. But now the time had come to stop all the nonsense.

"Rosita, you got to tell 'em where you hid that gold."

"No! I weel no tell. Tha' money ees my people. I weel take eet back to them."

"If you're dead, you can't take anythin' anywhere!"

"I don' care."

He put down the cloth. "Honey, Garrity said he's gonna give me five hundred dollars. I'll give you half of that. You can take it to your family. That's two hundred fifty for you and me both."

"No."

Slocum leaned against the wall. He wished he had some tobacco to roll. A smoke would have been a welcome diversion.

"We muz eescape," Rosita said.

Slocum scoffed. "Ain't even a window in this place. If I try to knock out a wallboard, they're gonna hear me."

She leaned against him. "Slocum, I love you."

"That's just dandy, Rosita. Plum damned dandy. We're both gonna be dead soon, so I reckon I'll see you on the other side."

Her head fell against his chest. "I sorry."

He touched her hair. "That was a pretty mean trick you played on me out there. Hittin' me with a rock and takin' off. You owe me, girl. So tell Garrity where to find that gold."

She did not reply. Instead, her fingers strayed to his crotch. Even with her sore back, she still did it with him. She sat on him, so her wound wouldn't hit the cot.

When they were finished, Slocum asked her again to tell Garrity where she hid the gold. The money wouldn't be any good to anybody if they were dead. At least they had a chance if she told Garrity where she had stashed the double eagles.

"You are no brave, Slocum."

He replied that bravery wasn't so important just now. When morning came and he couldn't tell Garrity where to find the gold, they would probably kill him. Rosita would have to go back to Mexico to endure more torture from Miguel. She'd be trapped forever.

The girl thought about it for a long time and finally agreed to tell him. "Eet's een the well behind the old mission. On a rope, hanging."

She reclined on the cot, lying on her side.

Slocum closed his eyes, waiting for sleep to come. He could tell his captors and get it over with in the morning. The tall man had no sense of the events that would prevent Garrity and Miguel from taking the gold. It never occurred to him that all hell might break loose at sunrise.

20

The stableman died just before dawn. His death rattle woke Slocum. He had been hit awfully hard by the Mexican.

Slocum hadn't even known the man's name. He had been helpful at times. Too damned helpful to Garrity and Miguel.

The lanky rebel leaned back against the wall.

Rosita opened her eyes a few moments later. "Slocum."

He had already decided to ask Garrity and Miguel not to kill her. They wouldn't want her blood after they had their money. They might want to kill Slocum, though.

"Mornin', girl."

She sat up, wincing in pain. The welt on her back had healed a little, but it still oozed some blood.

She put her head against his chest. "I dream bad dream."

Slocum thought the nightmare was just beginning.

The door opened.

Slocum looked up to see Garrity standing in the doorway. "It's gettin' close to daybreak."

Slocum did not move. "Garrity, I got to talk to you."

The chubby man stepped into the back room. He had his derringer in hand. "I warn you, Slocum, if you move, you're dead."

"That ain't it, Garrity. It's the girl. I want your word that nothin' more'll happen to her."

Garrity shrugged. "You take me to the gold, she'll be able to go back to Mexico with Miguel."

"No!" Rosita cried.

Slocum told her to be quiet. Going back to Mexico was better than dying. He looked at Garrity again.

"What now, Slocum?"

"Me, Garrity. What're you gonna do with me?"

A sigh from the fat man. "I been thinkin' about that, reb. You did the job and I could always use a man like that. I'm workin' on some things with the railroad in mind—"

Slocum squinted at him. "Mexican cattle and the railroad?"

"Yep. Seems there's talk that beef is gonna start goin' to market by train. I aim to get in on it. A man can make a lot of money on a newfangled thing, if it works."

Slocum thought he saw an opening. "Garrity, I meant to bring you every penny of that gold before this girl stopped me."

Rosita scowled at him. "You lie!"

"I mean it," the tall man went on. "When I was strung up on that rock, Red Buck put the gold with me. Gray Buck turned me loose with it. I was gonna bring it back here, but then I met up with the girl. She hit me with a rock. See the spot?" He turned his head. "Then she run off with the gold. I had to make her tell me where she hid it."

Rosita slapped at him. "Liar!"

Garrity waved the derringer. "Come on, Slocum, 'fore she beats you plum to death."

He rose off the cot. Garrity stepped backward through the door, keeping the derringer on him. He told Slocum to come out slow, put his hands behind his head, and stay real still.

The tall man obeyed him, watching for another opening.

Would he really be able to talk his way out of this thing? Garrity might change his tune once he saw all that gold.

Rosita started to come out of the back room.

"Stop her!" Garrity cried.

Slocum caught the girl and pushed her back, locking the door from the outside. She banged against the door, cursing him. Slocum turned to Garrity who told him to raise his hands again.

"You don't have to kill me, Garrity. Why should you? Everything worked out right. I delivered the cows. The bluecoats are gonna take care of Red Buck. Hell, you don't even have to give me five hundred. Just let me live."

Garrity started to say something, until he heard Miguel climbing down the ladder of the loft.

The Mexican came running to the rear of the stable. "The soldiers are awake."

Garrity nodded. "Good. They'll be gone soon. So will we."

Miguel looked at Slocum and then spat. "Greengo!"

Garrity frowned at the Mexican. "Aw, don't be like that, Miguel. I was thinkin' of askin' Slocum here to sign on with us."

"Af'er he stole your money!"

"There's no proof he stole it," the chubby man replied. "He said the girl took it. He had to rough her up to get her to tell him."

"No. We keel heem."

He turned away, heading for the loft again.

Garrity winked at Slocum. "Just get me to the gold, reb. I'll take care of Miguel."

Slocum wondered what kind of trick Garrity had up his oily sleeve. He could only go along with the chubby man for now. It was the best way to stay alive.

Colonel Barton sat his horse in front of his troops. The men had fallen into ranks on horseback. Miguel watched them from the loft. He could hear the colonel as he spoke.

"Men, you are going forth to face the hostiles. Their strength and numbers are equal to ours, though I am sure we will triumph. If you are all good soldiers, and I know you are, your weapons are ready. Your pistols and rifles are loaded. You will not bow to the hostile savages we are about to face. God will guide us and our hearts will be true."

Miguel grimaced at the old man's words. He watched as the snappy young lieutenant drew his saber and barked a command to the troops. They disappeared in a cloud of dust that diffused in the purple glow of daybreak.

The Mexican moved toward the ladder. He climbed down and nodded to Garrity. They led Slocum outside, keeping the rifle and the derringer pointed at his back.

Slocum strode toward the mission.

"Where are you going?" Garrity asked.

"The gold is in the well behind the mission," the tall man replied. "It's hangin' from a rope. The girl put it there."

"Wha' if he's lying?" the Mexican rejoined.

The chubby man lifted the derringer a little. "Then he gets it from both of us."

Slocum hoped the girl had told the truth. He knew Rosita would eventually be able to escape from Miguel. She was too resourceful to be held prisoner for very long. He wondered if he would be as lucky.

The soldiers had all gone north, so the mission was empty. They walked along the outside wall, turned the corner, and found the well. There was no bucket hanging over the ring of stones. It had to be dry.

"I don' see no money," Miguel said, scowling at the tall man. "The greengo lies."

Garrity wiped sweat from his forehead. "Give him a chance. Go on, Slocum. See what you can find. Don't forget that we got you covered. We're only gonna be a few feet away."

They followed him to the well, which appeared at first to have no ropes hanging from it. If Rosita had been lying, they would probably torture her until she revealed the true hiding place. Slocum knelt by the well, feeling with his fingers around the inside.

"You find it?" Garrity demanded.

Miguel was looking down at him. "There's no gold."

Sweat poured into Slocum's eyes. "Gimme a minute!"

Miguel prodded him with the rifle. "Liar!"

Slocum's hand hit something. "I got it." His fingers closed

around a thick section of rope. He tried to lift it with one hand, but it was too heavy.

"I need help," he said.

Miguel put the rifle on the ground and knelt next to him. "Eet ees heavy! Garreety!"

Slocum looked over at the man's smiling face. Miguel had the look of a successful thief in his dark eyes. He was also off balance.

Slocum grabbed his shoulder, pulling Miguel downward. The Mexican screamed as he tumbled into the well. He dropped a long way before he hit. A dull thud echoed out of the hole. The gold fell back into the well, bumping on the stones.

Garrity peered into the shadows below. "Miguel!"

Slocum rolled to his right, picking up the Mexican's rifle. He levered the Winchester and aimed it toward Garrity. The chubby man gawked at the rifle bore.

"Don't move, Garrity."

"Slocum, no! I was gonna shoot Miguel, anyway. Why do you think I winked at you in the barn?"

The tall man gestured with the rifle barrel. "Drop the derringer, Garrity; then we might talk."

Garrity's stubby fingers let go of the small pistol.

"Now, back away," Slocum told him.

When Garrity was a few feet behind the derringer, Slocum got up and grabbed the two-shot weapon. He put it in his pocket. He turned back to Garrity, swinging the Winchester.

"I got the drop now, fat man."

Garrity looked nervous. "You got it all wrong, Slocum. I wasn't gonna kill you, I swear."

"What were you gonna do, Garrity?"

"I figured the Mexican had it comin'. He wanted too much. But you were happy to take the five hundred. I knew you wouldn't back out on our deal, even if you—"

"Can it, Garrity. We got to get that gold out of the well."

The chubby man nodded, trying to smile. "I'm ready, Slocum. You want to help me?"

The tall man from Georgia gave a chortle. "No, I ain't gonna help you. Go on, get it."

"But it's heavy."

"Not that heavy. I just said that so Miguel would come down next to me. I reckon I surprised him."

Garrity moved next to the well. He looked into the hole. They could hear Miguel moaning at the bottom of the empty pit.

"Aw, shut up," Garrity said.

He picked up a large rock and threw it hard into the well. Miguel cried out, then was silent.

Garrity sweated bullets as he pulled up the rope.

The saddlebags came over the stone edge of the well. Garrity dropped them to the ground. Several gold coins spilled out into the dust.

The chubby man's eyes grew wide. "Look at it."

Slocum lifted the Winchester. "Don't forget, Garrity, I still have the rifle. I call the shots."

Garrity turned his face toward Slocum. "We had a deal," he said with newfound courage. "You were s'posed to bring back this gold to me. I only owe you five hundred. The rest is mine."

Slocum shook his head. "That's not how it is, Garrity."

"You can't kill me, reb. You're not a bushwhacker. You dealt straight with me all along. You can't shoot me."

"I don't plan to shoot you, Garrity. I—"

Slocum hesitated. He looked over his shoulder, then back at Garrity. Garrity heard it, too. A dull rumbling seemed to roll over the plain. It sounded like thunder.

"Look!" the fat man cried. "There!"

Dust rose on the plain. The noise grew louder. They could almost feel the ground trembling.

"What the hell is it?" Garrity asked.

"The soldiers," Slocum replied. "They're comin' back in a hurry. And I'm bettin' they're not alone."

"What—"

Slocum reached for the saddlebags. "Red Buck has—"

Garrity was suddenly on him, trying to hit him with his fists. "My gold, mine—"

The tall man swung the butt of the rifle into the man's gut. Garrity tumbled backward, teetering for a moment before he fell into the deep well. Slocum heard him slam into the stone below.

He grabbed the saddlebags, stuffing the fallen coins under the flap.

Suddenly the gold didn't seem as important to him. He lowered it back into the well and started to run hard toward the livery stable.

21

Slocum ran into the shadows of the stable. "Rosita!"

He remembered that she had been locked in the back room. When he let her out, she glared at him, at least until she heard the dreadful noise. Her eyes grew wide with fear.

"Wha'—"

Slocum handed her the derringer he had taken from Garrity. "The army's comin' back," he told her. "And they got Red Buck on their tails."

Rosita's hand began to tremble. "Slocum, I—"

He urged her toward the back room again. "Hide in there. Use the derringer if you have to."

"Slocum—"

He gave her a little push. "Go, woman."

The thundering grew louder outside.

Rosita stepped into the back room and closed the door. Slocum hadn't mentioned the obvious: If the Apaches were victorious, the girl should use the derringer on herself. It would be better to die than to end up as a squaw.

Slocum moved to the front door, cracking it so he could look out. Blue-coated soldiers rushed past the stable. Slocum frowned as the earth continued to tremble. Surely all the commotion could not be coming from the unshod ponies of Red Buck and his men.

The cavalrymen rode through town, out of Slocum's sight. He waited for the Apaches, holding Miguel's Winchester in hand. But to the tall man's surprise, the Indians did not come right away. Instead, a stampeding herd of cattle hit Pima's only street with a vengeance.

Red Buck had been smart. The renegade had driven the herd down from Apache Wells, using the cattle to chase the soldiers back to town. Slocum closed the door, latching it shut.

Outside, the cows rumbled in all directions. Some of them bounced against the stable. Slocum stayed by the door, waiting until the stampede had lost momentum.

The cattle still moved in the street, but they weren't running now. He opened the door again, peering out. Could the Apaches be far behind the herd? Or did Red Buck think the stampede alone would stop the soldiers?

Slocum peered toward the army outpost. He saw blue-coats moving around the side of the cabin. They seemed to be digging in for the attack. More soldiers were readying themselves on the porch of the general store. Slocum figured it would be best to join them. He could have run, but the tall man had a personal score to settle with Red Buck.

He left the stable and started across the street. The steers were crowding his way. Slocum pushed between the animals, turning his eyes to the north once in a while to see if Red Buck had arrived yet. The renegades had to be coming, otherwise why would the soldiers be digging in so deep? There were men on the roof of the general store and the mission. Slocum counted nine in all. Had the rest of the troop been decimated by the stampede?

He finally made it to the outpost.

The colonel and a sergeant drew pistols on him as he staggered through the front door.

"You!" the officer cried.

Slocum lifted his rifle. "One more gun, Colonel. Can you use another rifle in this thing?"

The colonel peered north, through the window of the outpost. "You were right, cowboy. Red Buck came after us."

Slocum shook his head. "I sure as hell didn't think he'd bring those cows with him."

Colonel Barton held an Army Colt in hand. "Believe it or not, Red Buck has made it easier for us."

Slocum couldn't bring himself to believe that statement. He levered the Winchester, making sure there was a round in the chamber. Then he gazed north, looking through the same window, waiting for the Apaches to ride into Pima.

The savages seemed to rise out of a dust cloud. There wasn't time to count them, but Slocum was pretty sure that Red Buck had brought his full force. The tall man used the butt of the rifle to break the glass in the window. He rested the rifle barrel on the sill, taking aim at the onrushing horde.

"Closer," the colonel said. "Come on, you renegade bastard."

Barton had a strange gleam in his eyes. He didn't seem to be afraid. Slocum wished he had the same confidence.

"Wait till they're in range," the colonel said. "Closer. We won't have to hold them off for long."

The rifles on top of the mission exploded first. A few of the Apaches fell, but the rest of them kept coming. Slocum tried to wait patiently, but he found himself squeezing the trigger out of fear.

"Wait on them!" Barton cried.

But they were almost on top of the outpost, as it was.

Slocum continued to fire.

Barton finally let his pistol erupt. The sergeant began to fire as well. Apaches surrounded them in a sudden rush. Arrows and rifle slugs slammed into the walls outside. More glass broke in the windows. Slocum wondered if they were all going to die.

The Indians had to stop when they reached the throng of cattle. The herd blocked the way through Pima. Slocum suddenly saw Red Buck in front of the window. He raised his Winchester, firing a shot that missed the big renegade.

"Damn!" He fired again but he was out of ammunition. "Colonel, you got any shells for this—"

Slocum stood up, peering out the window again.

"Yes!" Barton cried. "There it is."

A bugle call rose over the whooping of the hostile savages. It sounded like the signal for an attack. Slocum could barely see the cloud of dust that rose up to the west.

"What the hell is it, Barton?"

"Forty of my men," the colonel replied. "They circled around; now they'll attack these bastards from the flank. But we've still got to give them what for. There are rifle cartridges in my desk. Get them!"

Slocum reloaded the Winchester from the full box of shells in the colonel's desk.

"We've got them right where we want them," Colonel Barton boasted.

Slocum wasn't so sure. Still, he went back to the window, firing at the Apaches as fast as he could crank the lever of the Winchester.

The lanky man from Dixie thought it was a thing of beauty when the cavalry rode in on Red Buck's war party.

He saw Red Buck turn to glare at the approaching band of soldiers. Slocum shot at him again, but the slug missed the big renegade. Red Buck gave the order and the Apaches turned to face the onrushing cavalrymen.

"Don't stop shooting!" Colonel Barton cried. "Help our boys if you can."

Slocum pulled the trigger again.

The cavalry and the renegades collided a few hundred yards away from them. Slocum hesitated, gaping at the spectacle. Sabers flashed in the morning sun, rifles and handguns exploded. Soldiers and Apaches both fell into the dust. He levered the rifle again, wondering which army would win.

The cavalry seemed to be getting the best of Red Buck and his men.

Colonel Barton raised a fist in the air. "We've got 'em on the run."

Slocum squinted at the cloud that had risen over the skirmish. "I hope you're right, Barton."

It was hard to tell who was really winning, what with the cattle mixing in with the horsemen.

But the Indians kept falling until there didn't seem to be any more of them on horses. A few ran on foot, trying to get away, only to be cut down by the well-placed slash of a cavalry saber. Slocum stood there with his rifle, watching through the smoke and dust.

"We've done it," the colonel said. "We've—"

They both heard the cry from the savage throat.

"My God," the sergeant said.

Slocum lifted the rifle. He took aim at Red Buck, who was making one last charge at the outpost. The Apache's face was contorted in rage. He drove his pony hard toward the colonel.

Slocum pulled the trigger, but the Winchester jammed on him.

Colonel Barton raised his pistol too late.

The soldiers fired from outside, but they couldn't stop Red Buck from crashing through the window of the outpost.

When the renegade burst through the broken glass, he landed on the colonel. Immediately, the sergeant tried to grab Red Buck, but the Apache swung a knife that scrawled a crimson line across the soldier's throat. Slocum fumbled with the rifle lever, but the Winchester was jammed for good.

Red Buck let out a war whoop. He turned on the colonel again, raising the knife. Slocum leapt toward the savage, swinging the rifle butt at his head. Red Buck dodged the blow, but it kept him from killing Barton.

"Come on," Slocum said. "Lemme see how brave you are when you don't have your men to back you up."

Red Buck turned away from the colonel and began to stalk the tall man from Georgia.

When the Indian made another leap with the knife, Slocum swung the rifle again, but it didn't do any harm to the renegade. Red Buck seemed to fly straight through the blow. He landed right on top of Slocum.

Slocum's green eyes saw the knife blade that lifted above him. He reached up, grabbing Red Buck's wrist. The point of the knife flashed in front of his face. He felt the strength of the Indian's arm.

Slocum managed to roll to his left, taking the savage with him. He enjoyed the advantage for a few moments. His fist slammed into the scarred face, but the punches didn't seem to hurt Red Buck.

The Indian threw Slocum to the side, rolling him into the wall.

The tall man expected Red Buck to get on him again, but instead, the renegade went after the colonel. He hovered over Barton, raising the knife. Slocum scrambled to his feet in time to make a dive onto the Apache's broad back. Red Buck stumbled in a circle, trying to shake Slocum off.

"Do somethin', Barton!"

The colonel struggled to regain his balance.

Red Buck banged Slocum against the wall. The air rushed from the drifter's lungs. He felt a pain in his back. But he still held on, trying to keep a choke hold around Red Buck's throat.

Where the hell was the rest of the cavalry?

Red Buck went after Barton again. Even with Slocum hanging on to him, the Indian managed to back the colonel into the wall. He lifted the blade of the knife, ready to strike the bluecoat who was pinned against the logs.

"Barton!"

Slocum looked over the Indian's shoulder. He could see the pistol barrel as it came up. Barton had managed to wield the Army Colt.

Slocum closed his eyes.

The pistol exploded a few feet from his face.

Slocum felt the Indian's body go limp. He fell with the tall renegade. When he opened his eyes, he saw that Barton had shot Red Buck in the face. There was a big hole where the Indian's right eye had been.

Slocum scurried to his feet, looking down as the life twitched out of Red Buck's body. "You got 'im, Barton."

But the colonel had slumped to the floor as well. Red Buck had managed to stick the knife in the colonel's shoulder before he died. Slocum reached for the hilt of the blade, pulling it from Barton's flesh.

"Barton!"

The soldier's eyes drooped. "Pain—"

Before Slocum could say another word, the young lieutenant burst into the outpost. "Colonel Barton, we— My God, what happened?"

Slocum gestured to the dead renegade on the floor. "It's over, at least for him. If you got a doctor, get 'im on the colonel right away. That wound ain't as bad as it looks, but he could bleed to death if you don't get a bandage on that shoulder."

The lieutenant shouted through the broken window. Several more soldiers rushed to join him. One of the men began to tend the colonel's wounded shoulder.

Barton's eyes rolled up. "Good job, Lieutenant."

"Thank you, sir."

The colonel coughed a little. "I never would've made it if this man hadn't saved my life."

"What man, sir? The cowboy?"

"Yes, he— Awh, the pain—whiskey."

The lieutenant fetched the bottle of red-eye from the colonel's desk. He gave his superior officer a few nips to ease the ache in his shoulder. Barton raved on in a delirious tone, extolling the virtues of the cowboy who had saved his life.

But when the lieutenant turned back to congratulate Slocum on a job well done, the tall, green-eyed drifter had disappeared. Stepping to the front door, the junior officer peered into the street, trying to find Slocum in the confusion. Dust filled the air, cattle and dead bodies littered the street. He couldn't see the tall rebel anywhere. So he wheeled toward the colonel, trying to help the other soldiers save the man's life.

Slocum hurried out of the army post, running between the cows that still moved through Pima. He grabbed the reins of the first two Indian ponies that he saw, pulling them toward the stable. His heart pounded as he went through the door. What if the girl had been killed?

"Rosita?"

There was no answer from the back room.

When Slocum opened the door, the girl raised the derringer at him.

"Just me, honey."

She wrapped her arms around his waist. "Slocum, I love you!"

"No time for that, Rosita. We got to hightail it out of here."

Her dark eyes were wide. "The Indians!"

"They're mostly dead," Slocum replied, "but we still got to go."

He moved away from the girl, grabbing the saddle he had taken earlier from the general store. The Indian pony didn't want to accept the saddle at first, but Slocum convinced the animal that he was boss. He found another old saddle for the second pony. The deceased stableman wouldn't have anything to say about him borrowing the tack.

Rosita was right there beside him. "Slocum—"

"Come on, we got to go out the back way."

The ponies barely made it through the rear door. Slocum mounted up. Rosita needed help, so he had to climb down and boost her into the saddle. He could still hear the soldiers shouting to each other. He knew he had to flee before the army caught on to what he was doing.

"Stay here for a minute," he told the woman.

Rosita watched him ride toward the rear of the mission. She knew what he was after. When Slocum rode toward her again, he had the saddlebags slung in front of him. He had gone to get the gold.

She tried to say something to him, but the tall man just passed by at a full gallop. Rosita had two choices: stay or go. She turned the head of the Indian pony and drove hard to the south, following the tall man's dust.

22

Slocum rode hard for a long time before he slowed the Indian pony. He kept looking over his shoulder, half expecting the cavalry to follow him. But the soldiers must have had their attention focused on cleaning up after the battle. Slocum still felt shaky after the skirmish. It reminded him of the other war he had fought and lost.

Rosita's pony came out of his dust. She was covered with prairie chalk. Her face looked angry. She hadn't been too happy about their hasty departure.

"Slocum, you—"

He turned to ride away again, nudging the pony into an easy lope.

Rosita pulled up beside him. "Why you run?" she asked.

His hand patted the saddlebags in front of him. "If the army found out I had this gold, they'd never have let me go. Prob'ly woulda wanted me to take those cows north again.

But I've had enough of cattle and Injuns for a while."

She pouted, her dark eyes focused on the bags filled with gold. "They weel fin' you an' get the money."

He shook his head. "They don't know I got the gold. And if they do go lookin' for it, they'll ride north, to Red Buck's camp."

"Wha' of Garrity and Miguel?"

Slocum sighed. "Dead as doornails. Both of 'em in the bottom of that well where you stashed the gold."

"You keel them?"

"More or less."

They rode for a while in silence.

He knew what the girl wanted. She would only be happy if he took the gold back to Mexico, to give it to the peasants whose cows had been stolen. But Slocum wasn't about to surrender what he had worked so hard to have. He just rode on to the south, keeping the girl in the corner of his eye.

They stopped at dusk, making camp on the banks of the San Simon River. Slocum had left Pima without a weapon, so he could not shoot any game for dinner. Rosita was full of tricks, however. She managed to catch three large catfish from the clear waters of the San Simon. Slocum built a fire for her to cook the ugly creatures.

The fish tasted a little strong, but it filled Slocum's belly. He kept watching the girl. She had to make a move. It was in her nature.

Rosita took off her dress and washed in the waters of the river. When she was clean, she gave herself to Slocum in the light of the fire. The tall man took his pleasure, even though he had his suspicions. Afterward, they lay together on the saddle blankets.

Slocum closed his eyes, pretending to drift off to sleep. As soon as his bogus snoring began, the girl started to move. He could feel her trying to lift the saddlebags that lay beside him.

The tall man reached up to grab her wrist. "I knew it."

Rosita frowned. "No, Slocum—"

But he wasn't about to listen. She had stolen the gold from him once. He had no intention of giving her a second chance. Using leather strips from both saddles, he tied her hands and ankles together.

"Don' leave me!" she cried.

"I won't. But I need some shut-eye and I want to wake up to find my gold beside me."

It was his fortune, after all.

He rested easier knowing that the girl was tied. When he awoke at sunrise the next day, she was still there, glaring at him. He freed her and began to saddle the ponies.

"You are thief!" she cried.

Slocum figured he couldn't argue with that statement. It never did much good to argue with women, anyway. A man could never win a fight with a woman. If nothing else, she would always cry and make him feel like a shit-heel.

"Slocum!"

"I heard you the first time, Rosita."

When he had finished saddling the ponies, he mounted up, turning the animal's head south again.

Rosita called to him until she realized that she had better get into the saddle, too. Slocum didn't care if she rode with him, but he was sure as hell not going to lag on her account. She also knew that he was making for Mexico, which still gave her hopes for the gold. She refused to believe that Slocum was a bad man, even if he did seem intent on stealing the money.

The girl swung clumsily into the saddle, hanging on as the pony started toward the border. She managed to catch up with Slocum, to resume her arguments for the rightful redistribution of the stolen gold. But the tall man did not listen very closely. He had his plan. And he stuck to it, at least until they arrived again at the one-horse town called Dos Cabezas.

Slocum didn't want to stop at Dos Cabezas at first. But when he thought about the risk, it seemed small. Garrity and Miguel were no longer stomping around the territory and the soldiers were still busy in the north. What would it hurt to stop and have a good meal, a bath, and a real bed for a change?

Rosita was eager to stop in the town since she had kin there. Slocum figured he could ditch her once they split up.

He could head for California, where she would never think to look for him.

They walked the ponies down the lonely trail to the cantina. It was almost dark. Slocum dismounted in front of the cantina, slinging the heavy saddlebags over his shoulder. Rosita just kept riding on, which made him think he had seen the last of her. She didn't even turn around to bid him farewell.

Her coldness might have broken another man's heart, but Slocum had the gold to keep him company. He strode into the dark cantina. The place smelled of stale whiskey and peppers. A Mexican man looked up at him from behind a crude counter.

"Señor! Welcome."

Slocum nodded to the cantina man. "Need some grub, some whiskey, and a bath."

The man was eager to please his new customer. "Sí, señor. I have a tub in the back. Hot water weel cost more."

Slocum dug into his pocket, taking out a double eagle. He tossed the coin to the man, who snatched it from the air. The cantina man bit the gold to make sure it was real.

"That bath," the tall man said.

"Sí, señor. Pronto!"

Slocum shook his head, letting out a cynical laugh. Gold made every man your friend, at least until your pockets were empty. It was the way of the West, of the world. He figured to have it easy for a while. But then fate got in the tall man's way again.

Slocum eased his sore body into the hot water. His weight caused some of the bathwater to spill over the edges of the tub. He leaned back, glad that it was all finished. California awaited him and his fortune.

"Señor, ees there anythin' else you need?"

Slocum looked up at the little man who called himself Pepe. "Just some grub and whiskey, like I said."

"Sí. I ha' the good wheeskey. Fra' back east."

He started to go. Slocum stopped him. He asked Pepe if the Mexican man could find a gun for him.

"Wha' gun, señor?"

"Any gun," the tall man replied. "Rifle, pistol, shotgun. It has to shoot, but that's about it."

Pepe shrugged. "I can get for you, but weel cost."

"What kinda gun and how much?"

"Rifle—feefty dollar. Pistola—ten dollar. No shotgun. Pistola and rifle, seexty dollar."

Slocum nodded. "Go on."

"But your food, señor—"

"Later. I need the guns now. And bring as many shells as you can find. A holster, too."

"Weel cost more."

"Just bring 'em. I'll pay."

Pepe left in a hurry.

Slocum leaned back in the tub. His green eyes lifted to the saddlebags that rested against the wall. The guns would help him keep his fortune. He was glad he had stopped in Dos Cabezas.

He closed his eyes, sleeping for a while in the tub.

When he awoke, the water was cold and somebody was moving in the shadows.

Slocum sat up. "Pepe?"

He heard the clicking of a pistol cylinder.

"Hello, reb. Bet you thought you'd never see me again."

It took Slocum a moment to remember the voice. He could not see the face, but the hateful mouth was too damned familiar. Slocum started to stand up.

"Don't move, reb."

He hesitated, watching as the man came closer.

"Rattman, you bastard."

The outlaw held a pistol in his left hand. "You ruined my good gun hand, reb. So I'm gonna kill you."

"It doesn't have to be like that, Rattman. It never did. You forced me to shoot you. It was a fair fight."

"No, it wasn't!" Rattman cried. "You suckered me into drawing on you. But the worm has turned now."

Slocum figured he might have a chance in the shadows. Rattman could miss, since he wasn't shooting with his true gun hand. But a deal might be the smarter trail to ride. Slocum did have the gold to bargain with.

"Look here, Rattman, why don't we settle our business

without guns? I can pay you what you would have made from Garrity."

The outlaw laughed at him. "How is the old fat man?"

"Dead."

"You kill him?"

Slocum shook his head. "No. We had some Injun trouble. I got out with my life, but I did manage to escape with what Garrity paid me at the end of the drive. I can give you a hundred dollars."

Again Rattman laughed in his face. "I can take ever'thin' you got, reb, after I kill you. See, I don't care nothin' about the money. When I saw you ridin' into Dos Cabezas, I knew I'd get my revenge. Say hello to the devil for me, you gray-coat bastard. I'll see you in hell."

Slocum started to move, even though he figured it was the end.

He was halfway out of the tub when the pistol exploded. Only it wasn't Rattman's handgun that went off. Another weapon flashed in the shadows of the cantina.

Rattman's body buckled. He fell to the floor, wrestling himself to death. He was holding his head. Somebody had shot him in the temple.

Slocum hesitated, peering into the darkness. "Pepe?"

Someone struck a match, lighting a candle. The circle of flame moved closer to the tub. He saw Rosita behind the candle. She was holding the derringer he had given her in Pima.

She looked down at Rattman's body. "I keel heem."

Slocum squinted at the derringer. "You had that all along. You coulda shot me on the trail. Took your gold."

Rosita pointed the weapon at him. "No. I love you. I no keel you. I save your life. You are now een my debt."

He grimaced, shaking his head. He owed her, all right. And he was pretty sure he knew what she wanted.

"Rosita—"

"The gold, Slocum."

He sighed. "All right, honey. I'll do what you want. Just don't shoot me with that popgun."

She lowered the weapon. "I no shoot you. You do for me. No?"

He gave his word to her. He said he would do what she wanted. After all, she had saved his life and there was no way Slocum could turn his back on her now. Not for all the gold in Arizona.

23

The plaza of Pitiquito had been strung with festive banners and glowing lights. Torches also burned high and bright over the tiny Mexican village, staving off the night that had fallen on the celebration. Strains of Spanish music lilted in the warm air, reaching the ears of the tall drifter and the dark-eyed girl.

Rosita sat next to Slocum, watching the celebration. He had never seen her so happy. Her people had welcomed her back to Pitiquito. The gold had turned them all into forgiving souls.

Slocum had come south with her, crossing the border. All the way down, he had worried about the gold, but no trouble had come their way, not even when they arrived in Rosita's village.

Slocum had wondered how Miguel's former compañeros would look upon the death of their leader. The villagers were happy to hear of the Mexican's demise, since he would no longer be stealing their cattle. But the tall man had feared some sort of reprisal by Miguel's band of thieves.

Rosita took matters into her own hands, passing out the double eagles to keep the bandits happy. After all, she said, they had never been too keen about stealing from their own people. Fear of Miguel and high wages had swayed them to rustle every cow they could find south of the border. Now that their pockets were full of gold, they would leave the villagers alone for a while.

As for himself, Slocum was content with the five hundred dollars that Rosita had given him. She figured the amount to be fair, since it was the sum agreed upon in his original deal with Garrity. He hated to let his fortune go, but he decided that the money had been pretty much of a nuisance, anyway. Slocum was bound by his word to the girl, especially since she had saved him in Dos Cabezas. The peasants had their money and Slocum was paid off. There was nothing more to do but watch the festive celebration.

Firecrackers went off in the plaza. The music grew more lively and the Mexicans began to dance. Slocum sat with the girl next to him. Rosita sighed and leaned her head against his shoulder.

"Slocum, I love you."

The tall man from Georgia did not reply.

She looked into his eyes. "Do you hate me?"

"No."

"Theen you love me?"

He sighed. "Why don't you go dance with the others?"

She laughed. "I wan' dance wi' you."

"I can't get the hang of that Mexican stompin'."

She touched his chest with her hand. "No tha' dance. We dance een bed."

Slocum suddenly found himself agreeable.

Rosita got up, taking his hand. She led him through the fancy house that had once belonged to Miguel. There was a big bed in the hacienda. Slocum joined her on the clean white sheets.

They kissed until they became as hot as the night.

Slocum fumbled with the buttons of Rosita's dress until she knocked his hands away. As she disrobed, the tall man took off his own clothes. Rosita laughed as she tossed her dress on the floor. She fell next to Slocum and started to kiss him.

Her hand strayed to his crotch. Soft fingers closed around his stiffening manhood. Rosita stroked him until he was rock hard.

She reclined on her back, spreading her legs.

Slocum rolled on top of her, prodding with his prick. Rosita reached down to guide him in. Her body trembled when he entered her.

The Mexican girl turned into a wildcat that night. She humped and groaned, taking him through the paces. He did things he had never done to a woman before. And Rosita seemed to love it all.

An hour later, they collapsed on the bed.

Rosita snuggled next to him. "I so happy, Slocum."

He just grunted. He didn't want her to start talking. Once a woman got her lips flapping in bed, she couldn't be stopped.

Outside the hacienda, the celebration wore on. Voices rose up in a hymn of praise. Rosita listened carefully and then laughed.

"They seeng for you," she told Slocum. "You breeng the money. You ma' them happy."

The tall man was not impressed. No one had ever sung a song for him and most likely, they never would do it again. He closed his eyes to sleep, but the girl was not finished talking.

"Slocum, I love you. Stay wi' me. We leeve here, in theese hacienda. I can be your wife."

He did not reply. Maybe if he was quiet, she would go to sleep. The lanky rebel from Georgia had no desire to stay with Rosita in Mexico.

She wasn't ready to give up on the idea, however.

"Slocum—"

He put his finger on her lips. "Shh. Let's sleep some."

Her fingers rubbed his stomach. Slocum felt the stirring. He had to admit that she knew how to take care of a man. He could do worse for a wife. Only he hadn't been looking for one when he met Rosita. A drifter couldn't make a woman happy.

"Slocum," she cooed.

Her fingers stroked his cock to life.

He started to roll over on top of her again.

"No," she said. "No yet."

She kissed his chest, working her way down the line of his stomach. Slocum tensed when she put her mouth on his cock. She sucked him, licked his scrotum, stayed on him till he thought he would burst.

The tall man finally couldn't take it anymore. He rolled over on top of her and sank his cock into her. Rosita bucked again, humping on the bed like a raw bronco. Slocum released deep inside her, causing her to cry out with her own pleasure.

"I love you," she whispered.

He climbed off her, reclining on the bed.

Music continued to drift in from the celebration. He was afraid the girl would start talking again, but she closed her eyes instead. Slocum got off the bed when Rosita started to snore.

He looked down at her one last time. She was so damned beautiful. He was almost tempted to accept her offer to stay, but he knew the good time would turn sour sooner or later. She'd do her best to change him into a husband, and he'd resist. It would never work.

The tall man wheeled away from the bed, moving in the shadows. He gathered his clothes and dressed quietly. Rosita stirred in her sleep. He had a lie ready if she woke up. But she didn't.

Slocum headed toward the window that looked down on the street. He watched the celebration for a few moments. He should have felt better about helping the citizens of Pitiquito, but he could not forget the fortune he had lost. At best, he was numb from the whole thing. He wanted to get the hell out of Mexico, to forget the girl and her people.

Climbing out of the window, he dropped to the ground and made his way along the adobe wall. He ran for the stable in back of Miguel's old house. The tall man grimaced when he caught sight of the well behind the hacienda. It reminded him of Miguel and Garrity, two thieves who had died by his hand. There didn't seem to be a way to get rid of the killing, not if a man was going to ride the western territories.

His gear had been stored in the stable with his new horse. Slocum had used part of his money to buy a big, chestnut gelding. It reminded him of the horse that he had lost at Apache Wells when Red Buck attacked and killed the two boys. The renegade had been forced to pay for his crimes, so the slate was clean now.

The gelding snorted when Slocum came in. He saddled the animal, putting his shiny new Winchester on the sling ring of the saddle. His saddlebags were no longer full of gold, but he did have an Army Colt and a new holster. The cantina man in Dos Cabezas had gotten the weapons for him.

Leading the chestnut out of the stable, he mounted up and took one last look at the village. He thought about saying adios to the girl, but he didn't want to endure her tears. It was best just to leave. Sentimentality didn't fit well on the tall drifter from Georgia.

He turned the gelding to the north, driving for the border as fast as the animal would take him. Slocum wanted to try California for a while.

Drifting didn't feel good, but it didn't feel bad, either. The cool, night air rushed by him as he galloped north. He had to wonder how long it would be until trouble found him again. It was a risk he was willing to take.

The chestnut galloped on, leaving the girl and the Mexican village behind.

EPILOGUE

The California sun beat down on the tall man's head. He tipped his hat forward, covering his rugged face with the shade of the brim. Slocum's luck hadn't been good. He had already spent most of the money he had made in Arizona. The girl and the trail drive were out of his memory, but he could not forget the gold that had fallen through his fingers.

He cursed under his breath, thinking that things could not get any worse. Then the chestnut gelding went lame on him. Slocum had to shoot the poor creature before he walked on with his saddle on his shoulder.

It all came to nothing sometimes. No matter how much gold you had, it was easy to lose it to bad poker hands and loose women. Whiskey and beefsteak sat on the table of a wealthy man, but a poor man was always wondering where his next meal would come from.

Slocum's belly ached with that empty feeling. He walked until his body wanted to give out. He had to find shade then, to wait for the cool afternoon air to fall over the California landscape. Slocum figured he had seen enough of California for a while. But how the hell was he going to get away from the bothersome state?

He decided to sleep for a bit and then worry about it.

When Slocum opened his green eyes, he stared up at a shape that loomed against the afternoon sky. It had to be a white man or a Mexican. The figure wore a wide-brimmed sombrero. Slocum started to sit up. A rifle barrel poked him in the chest.

"What the hell you doin' on my land, boy?"

He squinted to see if he could make out the man's face.

"Go on, tell me why you're trespassin'."

Slocum exhaled. "Sir, my horse took up lame. I had to shoot 'im."

The man lifted the rifle from Slocum's chest. "I saw the dead animal. What kind was it?"

"Chestnut. Geldin'."

That seemed to satisfy the stranger. "Okay. But I want you to get the hell off my land. I find you here tomorrow, I'll shoot you."

He started away from Slocum.

The tall man scrambled to his feet. "Hey!"

The stranger turned back to him. "You got a problem?"

"I need work," Slocum replied.

"What kinda work you lookin' for?"

He shrugged. "Honest work. It doesn't matter."

A deep sigh from the stranger. "Okay, you want work. My ranch is west of here. That way."

He pointed with the rifle.

Slocum tried to force a smile. "Mind if I ride with you?"

The man shook his head. "Can't. You walk over. See the woman. She'll tell you what to do. If you hurry, you can get started before dark."

He got on his mount and rode off.

Slocum made a hateful gesture. "Thank you kindly."

He picked up the saddle and started to walk.

The ground rolled along in a series of ridges. Just when

Slocum figured he wasn't going to make it to the ranch, he saw the spread from the crest of the last rise. The ground leveled off into a basin that was covered with brush.

He walked on toward the ranch house, shuffling on tender feet.

Why had he ever let the girl talk him out of the gold?

He decided it was best not to torture himself.

If he could make it to the ranch house, the tall man figured he would live.

When Slocum stopped in front of the house, he heard a woman's voice telling him not to move. He glanced at a window and saw that she had a rifle pointed at him.

"Who the hell are you?" she demanded.

Slocum tipped back his hat, so she could see his dirty face. "My horse died," he told her. "Met a man 'bout two miles that way. Said you might have some work for me."

"What kinda man was he?" the woman asked.

He shrugged. "Had on a sombrero. Sort of mean-like. Said you had some work for me if I—"

"Stay right there," she said.

The woman disappeared from the window. She came onto the porch with the rifle in front of her. Slocum kept his hands high, so she wouldn't have an excuse to shoot him.

"You really want to work?" she asked.

Slocum nodded.

"All right. My name is Bessie. That was my brother you talked to. He'll be back in the mornin', but I know how to use this rifle, so don't get no ideas."

"I just want to work, ma'am. For food or money. It don't matter. If you got a horse I could—"

"Hush up a minute, let me think."

Slocum studied her round face. She had fair skin, soft cheeks. Her body was plump and Slocum was sure she had seen her thirtieth birthday come and go. He had been with worse-looking women. Bessie was probably a widow or an old maid.

"You ever put on a barn roof?" she asked.

Slocum nodded. "One or two."

Bessie pointed with the rifle, just like her brother. "Had some bad weather last month. Blew off our barn roof. Ain't had time to fix it just yet. You want the job, it's yours.

Pay you ten dollars when you're finished. Meals while you work. There's a old gray nag in the corral. You put that roof on, I'll throw it in."

Slocum accepted her offer. He went to work right away, hammering and nailing on the roof. It was still a hot afternoon, so he took his shirt off. As he worked from a ladder, he caught the woman staring at him from the window of the kitchen. Maybe she would throw in more than the money and the horse.

"Oww!"

Slocum grabbed his hand. The woman had distracted him into hitting his thumb. A dark bruise began to form under his thumbnail.

He cursed his miserable fate. Not two months earlier, his pockets had been full of money. How quickly he had fallen from grace.

Then he heard the door opening. He glanced toward the ranch house.

The woman had come out onto the porch. She was carrying a pitcher of lemonade. Her thin lips were drawn up in a curious smile. She started toward Slocum with the pitcher.

"Better have a drink," she called from the bottom of the ladder.

Slocum climbed down to wet his whistle. He caught her staring at the lines of his body, but he didn't want to rush her. He climbed up again, starting with the hammer. She could wait until dark. In the meantime, he planned to do a good job on the roof.

The tall man hammered and nailed, working hard until Bessie called him in to dinner.

A special offer for people who enjoy reading the best Westerns published today. If you enjoyed this book, subscribe now and get . . .

TWO FREE WESTERNS!
A $5.90 VALUE—NO OBLIGATION

If you enjoyed this book and would like to read more of the very best Westerns being published today, you'll want to subscribe to True Value's Western Home Subscription Service. If you enjoyed the book you just read and want more of the most exciting, adventurous, action packed Westerns, subscribe now.

TWO FREE BOOKS

When you subscribe, we'll send you your first month's shipment of the newest and best 6 Westerns for you to preview. With your first shipment, two of these books will be yours as our introductory gift to you absolutely FREE, regardless of what you decide to do.

Special Subscriber Savings

As a True Value subscriber all regular monthly selections will be billed at the low subscriber price of just $2.45 each. That's at least a savings of $3.00 each month below the publishers price. There is never any shipping, handling or other hidden charges. What's more there is no minimum number of books you must buy, you may return any selection for full credit and you can cancel your subscription at any time. A TRUE VALUE!

Mail the coupon below

To start your subscription and receive 2 FREE WESTERNS, fill out the coupon below and mail it today. We'll send your first shipment which includes 2 FREE BOOKS as soon as we receive it.